A Book Of

PHARMACEUTICAL INORGANIC CHEMISTRY

SIMPLIFIED

F. Y. B.Pharm [Semester - I]
As Per New Revised Syllabus

Dr. K. S. Jain
M. Pharm., Ph.D., FIC
Principal and Professor
Jain Vidya Prasarak Mandal's
Rasiklal M. Dhariwal Institute of Pharmaceutical Education and Research (RMDIPER)
Chinchwad Station, Pune 411 019

Dr. P. B. Miniyar
M. Pharm., Ph.D., FAGE
Professor and Vice-Principal
Sinhgad Technical Education Society's
Sinhgad Institute of Pharmacy, Narhe, Pune - 411 041

Mrs. P. V. Bhawar
M. Pharm.,
Assistant Professor
Jain Vidya Prasarak Mandal's
Rasiklal M. Dhariwal Institute of Pharmaceutical Education and Research (RMDIPER)
Chinchwad Station, Pune 411 019

NIRALI PRAKASHAN
ADVANCEMENT OF KNOWLEDGE

N1318

Pharmaceutical Inorganic Chemistry | **ISBN 978-93-5164-874-1**

First Edition : October 2015

© : Authors

Published By :

NIRALI PRAKASHAN

Abhyudaya Pragati, 1312, Shivaji Nagar,
Off J.M. Road, PUNE – 411005
Tel - (020) 25512336/37/39, Fax - (020) 25511379
Email : niralipune@pragationline.com

☞ **DISTRIBUTION CENTRES**

PUNE

Nirali Prakashan : 119, Budhwar Peth, Jogeshwari Mandir Lane, Pune 411002, Maharashtra
Tel : (020) 2445 2044, 66022708, Fax : (020) 2445 1538
Email : bookorder@pragationline.com, niralilocal@pragationline.com

Nirali Prakashan : S. No. 28/27, Dhyari, Near Pari Company, Pune 411041
Tel : (020) 24690204 Fax : (020) 24690316
Email : dhyari@pragationline.com, bookorder@pragationline.com

MUMBAI

Nirali Prakashan : 385, S.V.P. Road, Rasdhara Co-op. Hsg. Society Ltd.,
Girgaum, Mumbai 400004, Maharashtra
Tel : (022) 2385 6339 / 2386 9976, Fax : (022) 2386 9976
Email : niralimumbai@pragationline.com

☞ **DISTRIBUTION BRANCHES**

JALGAON

Nirali Prakashan : 34, V. V. Golani Market, Navi Peth, Jalgaon 425001,
Maharashtra, Tel : (0257) 222 0395, Mob : 94234 91860

KOLHAPUR

Nirali Prakashan : New Mahadvar Road, Kedar Plaza, 1st Floor Opp. IDBI Bank
Kolhapur 416 012, Maharashtra. Mob : 9850046155

NAGPUR

Pratibha Book Distributors : Above Maratha Mandir, Shop No. 3, First Floor,
Rani Jhanshi Square, Sitabuldi, Nagpur 440012, Maharashtra
Tel : (0712) 254 7129

DELHI

Nirali Prakashan : 4593/21, Basement, Aggarwal Lane 15, Ansari Road, Daryaganj
Near Times of India Building, New Delhi 110002
Mob : 08505972553

BENGALURU

Pragati Book House : House No. 1, Sanjeevappa Lane, Avenue Road Cross,
Opp. Rice Church, Bengaluru – 560002.
Tel : (080) 64513344, 64513355,Mob : 9880582331, 9845021552
Email:bharatsavla@yahoo.com

CHENNAI

Pragati Books : 9/1, Montieth Road, Behind Taas Mahal, Egmore,
Chennai 600008 Tamil Nadu, Tel : (044) 6518 3535,
Mob : 94440 01782 / 98450 21552 / 98805 82331,
Email : bharatsavla@yahoo.com

niralipune@pragationline.com | www.pragationline.com
Also find us on ⨍ www.facebook.com/niralibooks

Foreword ...

I have read the book "Pharmaceutical Inorganic Organic Chemistry - Simplified – F.Y.B.Pharm. (Sem. I) "written by Dr. K. S. Jain, Dr. P. B. Miniyar and Mrs. P. V. Bhawar, for Nirali Prakashan, Pune.

The authors have rich experience in teaching the subject with a few books already to their credit. This book has been written for the students of first year B. Pharm. and consists of 10 chapters following the revised syllabus of the first year B. Pharmacy course implemented by Savitribai Phule Pune University, with effect from the academic year 2015-16.

The style of presentation of this book is such that, it will not only give a deeper understanding of the subject, but also overcome the fright of the beginners for the subject. Keeping in mind the importance of the subject-Inorganic chemistry, the authors have indeed made the contents of the chapters very simple, lucid and easy to understand with figures, wherever required. I feel the book shall be liked by both the students, as well as, the subject teachers for its unique quality and style of presentation, lucid explanatory language, as well as, complete coverage of the syllabus.

There are question banks provided at the end of each chapter, which shall help the students to face the exams with much confidence.

I congratulate the authors for bringing out this book and wish them the very best in this endeavour.

Dr.M. T. Chhabria, M.Pharm., Ph.D., FICS
Principal& Professor, Pharmaceutical Chemistry
L. M. College of Pharmacy,
Navarangpura, Ahmedabad-380 009
Gujarat, INDIA

Preface ...

Great gratitude is expressed towards all students and teachers for such a great response and acceptance for our two text books, on Pharmaceutical Organic Chemistry for F.Y.B.Pharm (Sem. I & II) & for S.Y.B.Pharm. (Sem. III & IV), published by Nirali Prakashan last year and whose 2nd editions are now published. We are indeed enthralled and encouraged to undertake the drafting of yet another book entitled **"A Text book of Pharmaceutical Inorganic Chemistry-Simplified"** for F.Y.B.Pharm. in a much simple but, concise manner.

The history and importance of Inorganic Chemistry is much older than Organic chemistry. Pharmaceutical Inorganic Chemistry deals with inorganic compounds as pharmaceutical agents. However, in the curriculum of pharmaceutical sciences not many standard and quality textbooks are available on this subject, albeit with an exception of a few by foreign authors. As the subject is relegated mostly to the first year, where students are fresh and not much conversant with text books authored by foreign writers, the dearth for quality texts by native authors is surely observed. Thus, the need was felt to provide a textbook on this subject in simple, lucid language but, in concise manner.

Various topics covered are those specified in the syllabus of the S.P. Pune University, as well as, the course content of Pharmacy Council of India.

These include, (a) Introduction to pharmaceutical inorganic chemistry, pharmacopoeia and monographs, (b) Quality control and tests for purity, c) Limit tests for arsenic, heavy metals, lead, iron, chloride and sulphate and Pharmacopoeial Standards.

The scope of this text book further covers classification of Inorganic pharmaceuticals based on therapeutic classes with examples and uses, their definitions, preparation, properties, assay methods and uses. Some of the topics covered are: (a) gastrointestinal agents, (b) electrolytes, (c) mineral nutrients, (d) pharmaceutical aids, (e) expectorants, (f) emetics, (g) antidotes, (h) inhalants, (i) dental products, (j) topical agents, (k) water, etc. Each chapter is provided with a rich question bank in the end.

We are confident that this book too shall prove to be very useful and handy to the students and teachers of the subject.

– Authors

Date : 22nd October 2015 (Vijayadashmi)

Syllabus ...

UNIT I

Introduction to pharmaceutical inorganic chemistry, Different Pharmacopoeia and contents of individual monographs. Indian Pharmacopoeia - History and detail study of different volumes along with general notices, new inclusion/exclusion of compound monograph.

Sources of Contamination in Pharmaceuticals and Methods to Control: Various limit tests including chloride, sulphate, arsenic, lead, iron and heavy metals as per IP. Limits of insoluble matter, soluble matter, non-volatile matter, residue on ignition and ash values. Qualitative tests for alkali and alkaline earth metals.

Water: Water as universal pharmaceutical vehicle. Hardness of water, methods to remove hardness of water, different official waters and official control tests for water.

UNIT II

Gastrointestinal Agents:

Acidifying agents:

Dilute hydrochloric acid

Antacids: Classification of antacids, Aluminium Hydroxide Gel, Aluminium Phosphate, Basic Aluminium carbonate, Calcium Carbonate, Magnesium carbonate, Magnesium Hydroxide, Magnesium Trisilicate, Sodium Bicarbonate, Combination of Antacids.

Protectives and Adsorbents: Bismuth compounds, bismuth subcarbonate, Kaolin, Activated charcoal, pectin.

Saline Cathartics: Sodium phosphate, Sodium potassium tartarate, Magnesium carbonate, magnesium sulphate.

Electrolytes: Extra and intracellular ions: Chlorides, Phosphate, Bicarbonate, Na, K, Ca, Mg. Electrolytes used for replacement therapy, Calculation of mEq/l, mOsmol/l of electrolytes, physiological acid base balance. Electrolyte used in acid-base therapy, Electrolytes combination therapy. Sodium chloride injection, Ringer solution lactated, Ringer injections, sodium acetate, potassium bicarbonate, sodium citrate, sodium lactate, ammonium chloride, oral rehydration salts.

Essential and Trace Elements: Absorption, distribution, physiological role. Official compound of Fe, Cu, Zn, I, Fe: Ferrous sulfate, Iron sorbitex injection, ferric ammonium citrate, ferric chloride, Cu: Copper sulfate, Iodine, Potassium iodide, Sodium iodide, Zn-Zinc sulphate.

UNIT III

Topical Agents:

General introduction and mode of action.

Protectives: Talc, zinc oxide, Calamine, Zinc stearate, Titanium dioxide, aluminum compounds.

Antimicrobials and Astringents: Hydrogen peroxide solution, Sodium perborate, Zinc peroxide, Potassium permanganate, Sodium hypochlorite, Iodine solution, Boric acid, Selenium sulfide, Zinc sulfate.

Dental Products: Dentifrices, Anti-caries agents.

Gases and Vapours: Important inorganic gases used in Pharmacy.

Oxygen, Nitrogen, Nitrous oxide ,Carbon dioxide, Helium, Ammonia and their compounds as per I.P.

UNIT IV

Miscellaneous Agents

✍ ✍ ✍

Contents ...

1. **Introduction to Pharmaceutical Inorganic Chemistry** 1.1 - 1.16

2. **Sources of Contamination in Pharmaceuticals and Methods to Control** 2.1 - 2.18

3. **Water** 3.1 - 3.8

4. **Gastrointestinal Agents** 4.1 - 4.20

5. **Electrolysis** 5.1 - 5.16

6. **Essential and Trace Elements** 6.1 – 6.18

7. **Topical Agents** 7.1 – 7.18

8. **Dental Products** 8.1 – 8.8

9. **Gases and Vapours: Important Inorganic Gases Used in Pharmacy** 9.1 – 9.8

10. **Miscellaneous Agents** 10.1 – 10.10

Chapter **1** ...

Introduction to Pharmaceutical Inorganic Chemistry

Contents ...

1.1 Pharmaceutical Chemistry
    1.1.1 Inorganic Chemistry
    1.1.2 Importance of Inorganic Pharmaceuticals
1.2 Pharmacopoeia
    1.2.1 History of Pharmacopoeia
    1.2.2 Indian Pharmacopoeia
    1.2.3 Indian Pharmacopoeia 2010
    1.2.4 Indian Pharmacopoeia 2014
    1.2.5 British Pharmacopoeia
    1.2.6 European Pharmacopoeia
    1.2.7 Pharmacopoeia International
    1.2.8 United States Pharmacopoeia (USP)
1.3 Official Monograph
1.4 New Inclusion / Exclusion of Monograph
• Question Bank

1.1 Pharmaceutical Chemistry

Pharmaceutical Chemistry is a branch of chemistry that deals with the chemical, biochemical and pharmacological aspects of drugs. It includes synthesis/isolation, identification, structural elucidation, structural modification, structural activity relationship (SAR) studies, study of the chemical characteristics, biochemical changes after drug administration and their pharmacological effects.

1.1.1 Inorganic Chemistry

Inorganic chemistry is the study of all the elements and their compounds except carbon and its compounds (which is studied under organic chemistry). Inorganic chemistry describes the characteristics of substances such as nonliving matter and minerals which are found on the earth except the class of organic compounds.

Branches of inorganic chemistry include coordination chemistry, bioinorganic chemistry, organometallic compounds and synthetic inorganic chemistry. The distinction between the organic and inorganic is not absolute, and there is much overlap, especially in the organometallic chemistry, which has applications in every aspect of the pharmacy, chemical industry–including catalysis in drug synthesis, pigments, surfactants and agriculture. In short, inorganic chemistry is the branch of chemistry that deals with inorganic compounds. In other words, it is the chemistry of compounds that do not contain hydrocarbon radicals (mainly C and H elements).

1.1.2 Importance of Inorganic Pharmaceuticals

Inorganic pharmaceuticals are useful in any of the following ways.

1. Useful medicinally for their therapeutic purpose. Example: Astringents, antimicrobials, etc.

2. Useful as pharmaceutical aids. Example: Bentonite, talc, etc.

3. To change the reaction of the body fluids i.e., to acidify or alkalise. Example: Antacids, alkalis, mineral acids.

4. Replacing or replenishing the normal content of body fluids. Example: Sodium, potassium, calcium, chloride, phosphate, etc.

5. Useful as reagents to carry out the reactions. Example: Catalysts (platinum, nickel) oxidising ($KMnO_4$) and reducing agents ($LiAlH_4$).

6. Useful in pharmaceutical analysis. Example: Titrants such as potassium permanganate etc.

1.2 Pharmacopoeia

The word Pharmacopoeia is derived from Greek words **'pharmakon'** means a drug (both remedy and poison) and **'poiein'** means to make or create. Pharmacopoeia is a book containing directions for the identification of samples and the preparation of compound medicines, and published by the authority of a government or a medical or pharmaceutical society. For this reason Pharmacopoeia is a legislation of a nation which sets standards and mandatory quality indices for drugs, the raw materials used to prepare them and the various pharmaceutical preparations

1.2.1 History of Pharmacopoeia

Each country has legislation on pharmaceutical preparations which sets standards and required quality indices for medicament, raw materials and preparations employed in the manufacture of drugs. These regulations are presented in separate articles. General and specific matters relating to individual drugs are published in the form of a book called a *Pharmacopoeia*.

On 15th December 1820, the first United State Pharmacopoeia (U.S.P) was released. In 1864, the first British Pharmacopoeia (B.P) was published with inclusion of monographs on benzoic acid, gallic acid, tartaric acid, tannic acid, camphor, lactose, sucrose and seven alkaloids along with their salts

1.2.2 Indian Pharmacopoeia

The Government of India constituted a permanent Indian Pharmacopoeia Committee in 1948 under chairmanship of Col. R. N. Chopra for the preparation of the Indian Pharmacopoeia and established a central Indian Pharmacopoeia Laboratory at Ghaziabad, Uttar Pradesh to keep it up to date.

The Indian Pharmacopoeia is published in fulfillment of the requirements of the Drugs and Cosmetics act, 1940 and rules there under.

Based on the recommendation of Indian Pharmacopoeial committee, the first edition of the Indian Pharmacopoeia (I.P) was published in the year 1955 under the chairmanship of Dr. B. N. Ghosh.

Supplement for the first edition of Indian Pharmacopoeia was published in the year 1960. This Pharmacopoeia contained both western and traditional system drugs commonly used in India. The same policy was continued while preparing the second edition of Indian Pharmacopoeia in 1966 with some modifications under the chairmanship of Dr. B. Mukherji. The supplement to the second edition of Indian Pharmacopoeia was published in 1975.

In view of the rapid advances and phenomenal growth in Indian pharma industry in early 1970, it was decided to publish a new edition of the pharmacopoeia and its addendum at regular and shorter intervals for which the Indian Pharmacopoeia Committee was reconstituted in 1978.

The third edition of the Indian Pharmacopoeia was published in 1985 under the chairmanship of Dr. Nityanand. Addendum/supplement I and II to the third edition were published in 1989 and 1991, respectively. In this Pharmacopoeia, inclusion of traditional system of drugs was made.

The fourth edition was published eleven year later, followed by the addendums published first in 2000 and the in 2002 and 2005. In addition, supplement 2000 for veterinary products were also released. The addendum 2005 was published by the Indian Pharmacopoeia which covered medicinal products not covered by any other Pharmacopoeias and attracted much global attention.

The Indian Pharmacopoeia Committee decided to delete the obsolete or less used product monographs and added monographs based on the therapeutic merit, medicinal need and their extent of use in the country.

The Indian Pharmacopoeial Commission (IPC) was established in the year 2005. The IPC provided systematic approach and practices for publication of Indian Pharmacopoeia 2007 with focus on those drugs and formulations that covered the national healthcare programmes and the national essential medicines. It contained monographs on antiretroviral, anticancer, anti-tubercular and herbal drugs. It further emphasised on biological monographs such as vaccines, immunosera for human use, blood products, biotechnological and veterinary (biological and non biological) preparations. Addendum 2008 to the Indian Pharmacopoeia 2007 was published which had taken care of the amendments to Indian Pharmacopoeia 2007 and also incorporated 72 new monographs.

The sixth edition of Indian Pharmacopoeia published in accordance with the principles and designed plan decided by the scientific body of the IPC. To establish transparency in setting standards for this edition, the contents of new monographs, revised appendices and other information have been published on the website of IPC, besides following conventional approach of obtaining comments.

The Indian Pharmacopoeia 2010 has been considerably revised and improved with respect of the requirements of monographs, appendices and testing protocols by introducing advanced technology.

The contents of appendices are by and large revised in line with those adopted internationally. The monographs of special relevance disease of this region have been given special attention.

Table 1.1 : Features of various Editions of Indian Pharmacopoeia

Sr. No. of Edition	Year of publication	Name of Chairman	Year of addendum released	Features of edition
First	1955	Dr. B. N. Ghosh	1960	Contains both western and traditional system drugs commonly used in India.
Seconds	1966	Dr. B. Mukherjee	1975	Contains both western and traditional system drugs commonly used in India.
Third	1985	Dr. Nityanand	1989 (1st) 1991 (2nd)	In this Pharmacopoeia inclusion of traditional system of drugs was limited. However, most of the new drugs manufactured and/or marketed were included while only those herbal drugs which had definite quality control standards had got place in it.

... (Contd.)

Sr. No. of Edition	Year of publication	Name of Chairman	Year of addendum released	Features of edition
Fourth	1996	Dr. Nityanand	2000 (1st) 2002 (2nd) 2005 (3rd)	It focuses on those drugs and formulations that cover the National Health Care Programmes and the National essential medicines. It contained monographs on antiretroviral, anticancer, anti-tubercular and herbal drugs. It further emphasised on biological monographs such as vaccines, immunosera for human use, blood products, biotechnological and veterinary (biological and non biological) preparations
Fifth	2007	Mr. Prasanna Hota (until 30 October 2006) and Mr. Naresh Dayal (from 31 October 2006)	2008	It is presented in 3 volumes : • Volume I contains general notices and general chapters. • Volumes II and III contains general monograph and drug substances dosage forms and pharmaceutical aid.
Sixth	2010	Mr. P. K. Pradhan	2012	It comprises of three volumes. Each volume has got different features. Volume I comprises notices, preface, about Indian Pharmacopoeia Commission, acknowledgements, introduction, general chapters and reference data.

				Volume II contains general notices, dosage forms (general monographs), drug substances, dosage forms and pharmaceutical aids (A to M). Volume III includes general notices, drug substances, dosage forms and pharmaceutical aids (N to Z), vaccines and immunosera for human use, herbs and herbal products, blood and blood related products, biotechnology products, veterinary products and index
Seventh	2014	Mr. Keshav Desiraj (until February 2014) and Mr. Lov Verma (February 2014 onwards)	2015	It is presented in four volumes. It included products of biotechnology, indigenous herbs and herbal products, veterinary vaccines and additional antiretroviral drugs and formulations, inclusive of commonly used fixed-dose combinations. Standards for new drugs and drugs used under National Health Programmes are added and the drugs as well as their formulations which are not in use now a days are deleted from this edition. The IP 2014 incorporates 2548 monographs of drugs, among these 577 are new monographs consisting of APIs, excipients, dosage forms, antibiotic monographs, insulin products and herbal products etc. 19 New Radiopharmaceutical Monographs and 1 general chapter is being included in this edition for the first time.

1.2.3 Indian Pharmacopoeia 2010

The new edition of Indian Pharmacopoeia entitled sixth edition (Indian Pharmacopoeia 2010) was published by the IPC. It supersedes the fifth edition but any monograph of the earlier edition that does not figure in this edition continues to be official as stipulated in the second schedule of Drugs and Cosmetics Act, 1940.

Presentation

The Indian Pharmacopoeia 2010 comprises of three volumes. Each volume has different features.

Volume I : Comprises notices, preface, about the Indian Pharmacopoeia Commission, acknowledgements, introduction, general chapters and reference data.

Volume II : Contains general notices, dosage forms (general monographs), drug substances, dosage forms and pharmaceutical aids (A to M).

Volume III : Includes general notices, drug substances, dosage forms and pharmaceutical aids (N to Z), vaccines and immune sera for human use, herbs and herbal products, blood and blood related products, biotechnology products, veterinary products and index.

The scope of Pharmacopoeia has been extended to include products of biotechnology, indigenous herbs and herbal products, veterinary vaccines and additional antiretroviral drugs and formulations, inclusive of commonly used fixed dose combinations.

Standards for new drugs and drugs used under National health programmes are added and the drugs as well as their formulations not in use nowadays are omitted from this edition. The number of monographs of excipients, anticancer drugs, herbal products and antiretroviral drugs has been increased in this edition.

Monographs of vaccines and immune sera are also upgraded in view of the development of latest technology in the field. A new chapter on liposomal products and a monograph of liposomal Amphotericin B injection is added advantage in view of latest technology adopted for drug delivery. A chapter on NMR is incorporated in appendices. The chapter on microbial contamination is also updated to a great extend to harmonise with prevailing International requirements.

Basis of Pharmaceutical Requirements

This compendium provided a statement concerning the quality of a product that can be expected and demonstrated at any time throughout the accepted shelf life of the article. The standards laid down represent the minimum with which the article must comply and is manufactured in accordance with then GMPs.

Also it is essential that sufficiently stringent limits are applied at the time of release of a batch of a drug substance or drug product so that the pharmacopoeial standards are met until its expiry date when stored under the storage conditions specified.

Valid interpretation of any requirement of Indian Pharmacopoeia has to be done in the context of the monographs and where appropriate, the specified tests and methods of analysis including any reference to relevant general notices to be performed. Familiarity with the general notices will facilitate the correct application of the requirements.

Changes

General chemical tests for identification of an article have been almost eliminated and the more specific infrared and ultraviolet spectrophotometric tests have been given emphasis.

The concept of relying on published infrared spectra as a basis for identification has been continued. The use of chromatographic methods has been greatly extended to meet the need for more specificity in assays and in particular, in assessing the nature and extent of impurities in drug substances and drug products. Most of the existing assays and related substances tests are upgraded by liquid chromatography method in view to have more specificity and to harmonise with other International Pharmacopoeias.

The test for pyrogens involving the use of animals has been eliminated. The test for bacterial endotoxins introduced in the previous edition is now applicable to more items. The test for abnormal toxicity is now confined to certain vaccines.

1.2.4 Indian Pharmacopoeia 2014

Highlights

- It is effective from 1st January, 2014

- Presented in 4 hard bound volumes with DVD

- Total monographs 2548 and 577 new monographs included

- For the first time in this edition 19 new radiopharmaceutical monographs and 1 general chapter is included

- Presented in user friendly format and cross referencing has been avoided

- Veterinary products monographs are the integral part of this edition

- Use of chromatographic methods has been greatly extended

- More specific IP and UV Spectrophotometer tests have been introduced and classical chemicals tests for identification of an article have been almost eliminated

- Test for pyrogens almost eliminated

- Obsolete monographs have been omitted

- More herbal drugs monographs have been added

- Several new monographs which are not present in any other major pharmacopoeias of the world are included

1.2.5 British Pharmacopoeia

In the year 1864, the first British Pharmacopoeia was published by combining the three old and reputed Pharmacopoeias namely Pharmacopoeia Londinensis (1618) Edinburgh Pharmacopoeia (1699) and Dublin Pharmacopoeia (1807). The 2nd edition was released in 1867.

The 3rd and 4th editions were published in the year 1885 and 1898, respectively.

Addendum to 2nd and 3rd editions were released in the year 1874 and 1890, respectively. Separate parts such as preparation of compounds were included in the 1864 British Pharmacopoeia. The contents were arranged alphabetically. In Britain it was realised that technical complexity of drug specifications was increasing and a different kind of set up was needed to prepare the Pharmacopoeias after publication of the fifth edition British Pharmacopoeia in 1914.

The next editions were published in 1928 and 1932. There after the commission was recommended to revise the British Pharmacopoeia once in every ten years. A range of diagnostic materials was included in the 1932 revision.

An important addition was inclusion of standards and tests for antitoxins and insulin. Seven addenta covered the interim edition between 1932 and the next edition of 1948. In this 1948 edition (7th), for substances newly introduced into medicine, generic names were provided. Methods of analysis such as disintegration tests for tablets and sterilisation methods were expanded. Many new monographs related to sex hormones and penicillins were also included.

Due to the rapid pharmaceutical and pharmacological progress at this time it was decided that the normal interval between new editions should be five instead of ten years.

The next edition was released in the year 1953. In this edition of British Pharmacopoeia, the titles of drugs and preparations were in English instead of Latin. Abbreviated Latin title was retained as a synonym. Capsules, constituted as new group of formulation and the implant methods for sex hormones and their standards were also described in this edition.

The 9th edition (1958) contained 160 new monographs. Spectrophotometric analysis and inclusion of tranquillising drugs were the other features of this edition. The next (i.e., 10th edition) was published in 1963.

The duties of the British Pharmacopoeia commission were defined clearly in Medicines Order 1970. The first edition of British Pharmacopoeia was prepared strictly under the provisions of Medicines Act and the 13th edition was published in the year 1980. Due to an expansion of drug information the British Pharmacopoeia was decided to be published in two volumes.

Standards for the quality of many substances, preparation and articles used in medicine and pharmacy for some 130 years were provided in 1993 edition of British Pharmacopoeia. For the convenience of the user this edition consolidated and extend the 1988 edition with its 1989, 1991, and 1992 addenta. Moreover monographs of the European Pharmacopoeia were also included in this particular edition.

The British Pharmacopoeia i.e., British Pharmacopoeia 2013 comprised of six volumes containing nearly 3,000 monographs for drug substances, excipients and formulated preparation, together with supporting general notices, appendices (test methods, reagents etc.) and reference spectra used in the practice of medicine in 5 volumes.

Also a single volume of the British Pharmacopoeia (Veterinary) 2013, along with a fully searchable CD-ROM and online access which provided flexible resources was provided.

The British Pharmacopoeia 2013 contained 41 new British Pharmacopoeia monographs, 40 new European Pharmacopoeia monographs, 619 amended monographs, 6 new and 1 amended infrared reference spectra and European Pharmacopoeia 7th edition material up to and including Supplement 7.5. In addition updates in January, April and July to harmonised with the European Pharmacopoeia were also provided.

The latest edition of the British Pharmacopoeia i.e., British Pharmacopoeia 2014 comprises five volumes and a single volume of the British Pharmacopoeia (Veterinary) 2014, along with a fully searchable CD-ROM and online access to provide with flexible resources.

Highlights of British Pharmacopoeia 2014

- Legally effective from 1st January 2014
- 40 new BP monographs are included
- 272 amended monographs
- Three new supplementary chapters are included
- Four new BP (Vet) monographs are included
- One new BP (Vet) supplementary chapter is included
- Free in-year updates in April and July to harmonise with the European Pharmacopoeia

1.2.6 European Pharmacopoeia

An official book of standards adopted by Germany, France, Italy, Netherlands, Switzerland and Belgium is the European Pharmacopoeia. In July 1964, the council of Europe issued an order, to frame out European Pharmacopoeia.

From 1969 onwards in the respective member countries it appeared as official standard book for medicinal substances and other drugs.

1.2.7 Pharmacopoeia International (International Pharmacopoeia)

In various countries there is no uniformity in terminology and strengths of pharmaceutical preparations used. In the year 1874, a view had been expressed that some world uniformity in the standards for potent drugs must be necessary to overcome various problems. These views were further endorsed in second International conference held in 1925 where an International agreement on the Unification of formulae for seventy seven potent drugs and preparations were reached. In 1936 the Health Organisation of the League of Nations established a technical commission of Pharmacopoeial experts.

The work was undertaken by the WHO after the World War II ended in 1946. Finally, volume I of the International Pharmacopoeia was published in 1951 in Latin with translations in English and French.

This International Pharmacopoeia contained monographs for over two hundred drugs and chemicals, with appendices on reagents tests and biological assays. Latter in the year 1955 the second volume was published which contained formulae for preparations having various drugs and substances already present in volume I.

In 1959 the supplement for 1st edition was released with incorporation of some newer drugs and substances with its method of preparations and the appropriate tests.

In 1967 the 2nd edition of International Pharmacopoeia was published, followed by a supplement in 1971. 3rd edition of International Pharmacopoeia was published in the form of several volumes, of which volume I appeared in 1979.

1.2.8 United States Pharmacopoeia (USP)

In 1817, Dr. Lyman Spalding proposed a plan to publish a National Pharmacopoeia to the medical society of the country at New York. On 15th December 1820 the first edition of United States Pharmacopoeia was published with 217 drugs in about 272 pages.

After the gap of ten years further editions of USP appeared. The 19th edition of USP was published in the year 1905. However, it was given the title of USP VIII as to show that it was 8th revision.

Pharmacopoeia must be revised every 5 years was suggested in the 1940 convention. On July, 5th 1974, unification of the USP and NF (National Formulary) was announced. Afterwards in the subsequent editions consolidated USP and NF into a single volume were published. USP covers all drug substances and drug products; whereas NF covers only pharmaceutical ingredients.

In January 1990, the 22nd edition of USP combined with 17th edition of NF was published. The current version of USP–NF standards deemed official by USP are enforceable by the United States Food and Drug Administration (US-FDA) for medicines manufactured and marketed in the United States.

The latest edition, USP 36–NF 31, published on November 1, 2012 in English, and became official from May 1, 2013. It contains more than 4,600 monographs with specifications for identity, strength, quality, purity, packaging, and labeling for substances and dosage forms. It also comprises more than 260 general chapters providing clear, step-by-step guidance for assays, tests, and procedures. Moreover it also focuses on specific charts and a combined index which help us to find the information.

1.3 Official Monograph

The monograph in a pharmacopoeia are the treatises on drugs and formulations which give description, assay, assay limits and other details necessary for maintaining requisite standards.

A monograph in I.P. includes the following.

1. **Title:** The main title for a drug substance is the International Non-proprietary Name (INN) approved by World Health Organization (WHO). The official name of the compound in english is stated in the title. In place of the main title, sometimes sub titles are given which are synonyms/subsidiary names; where included, they have the same significance as the main title. For example, calcium carbonate can also be called precipitated chalk; iron and ammonium citrate can also be called ferric ammonium citrate.

2. **Chemical formulae:** When the chemical structure of an official substance is known or generally accepted, the graphic and molecular formulae are normally given at the beginning of the monograph for information. To specify the absolute stereo chemical configuration International Union of Pure and Applied Chemists (IUPAC) systems have been used.

3. **Atomic and molecular weight:** The atomic and molecular weights are shown, as and when appropriate at the top right hand corner of the monograph. For example, magnesium chloride (Molecular weight: 202.30).

4. **Definition:** The opening statement of a monograph is one that constitutes an official definition of the substance, preparation or other article that is the subject of the monograph.

6. **Category:** This part of the monograph expresses the pharmacological or therapeutic or pharmaceutical application of the compound. Although the compound may have other applications usually this part describes the main application. Analgesics, antibiotics, antacids, laxatives etc. are some of the main categories for inorganic pharmaceuticals in the Pharmacopoeia.

7. **Dose:** Dose mentioned in the Pharmacopeia is intended merely for general guidance and represent, unless otherwise stated, the average range of quantities which are generally regarded as suitable for adults when administered by mouth. It provides the quantity guidance to the prescriber or the physician to achieve the desired therapeutic effects in adults. The dose can be altered as and when required. For example the dose of calcium carbonate is 1 – 5 gm.

8. **Usual strength:** It indicates the strength(s) usually marketed for information of the pharmacist and the medical practitioner.

9. **Description:** It illustrates a physical description of the substance such as amorphous nature or crystalline, odour, colour and taste etc. In the preliminary evaluation of the integrity of an article these properties help the standards in tests for purity.

10. **Solubility:** The solubility mentioned in Indian Pharmacopeia is the approximate solubility at a temperature between 15 °C and 30 °C. Different degrees of solubility are.

Very soluble	In less than 1 part
Freely soluble	In 1-10 parts
Soluble	In 10-30 parts
Sparingly soluble	In 30-100 parts
Slightly soluble	In 100-1000 parts
Very slightly soluble	In 1000-10,000 parts
Insoluble	In more than 10,000 parts

11. **Test methods:** References to general methods of testing are indicated by test method numbers in brackets immediately after the heading of the test or at the end of the text.

12. **Identification:** This usually involves specific chemical test or tests for identifying the substance. In general for inorganic pharmaceuticals, colour reactions, precipitation reactions and gas evolving reactions are used. For example, phenol gives violet colour with ferric chloride.

Some identification tests includes.

   I.   Infrared absorption spectroscopy

   II. Ultraviolet – visible spectroscopy

   III. Melting point or Boiling point

   IV. Simple chemical tests leading to formation of colour or precipitates

13. **Tests and assay:** These are the official methods upon which the standards of Pharmacopoeia depend. The requirements are not framed to take into account all possible impurities. Tests and assays are prescribed for the minimum sample available on which the attributes of the article should be measured.

14. **Limits:** These are tests designed to identify and control small quantities of impurities which are likely to be present in a substance. The limits given are based on data obtained in normal analytical practice. They take into account normal analytical errors, of acceptable variations in manufacture and of deterioration to an extent that is acceptable. No further tolerances are to be applied to the limits for determining whether or not the article under examination complies with the requirements of the monograph.

15. **Assay:** An assay gives in detail the analytical method for the substance in order to determine the percentage content of a particular chemical in the given test sample. The reagent required for assays and tests are defined in the appendices showing their nature, degree of purity and strengths of solutions.

16. **Storage:** The storage directions are useful in preserving the activity of the chemical. The terms used are well closed container, light resistant container, single dose container. I.P. also prescribes conditions for storage.

Cold	Between 2-8°C
Cool	Between 8°C – 25°C
Room Temperature	Temperature of working area.
Warm	30-40°C
Excessive heat	Above 40°C

17. **Storage containers:** The storage containers in the Pharmacopoeia are indicated in the following terms;

   (a) Well closed containers: This implies the substance is stable and gets protected from dust, dirt, insects etc, getting into the container.

   (b) Tightly closed container: The substances in such cases get affected by atmospheric oxygen or moisture or carbon dioxide

   (c) Light resistant container: Substances which are affected by light are stored in amber or dark colored containers

   (d) Single dose containers

18. Labeling: The labeling of drugs and pharmaceuticals is governed by the Drugs and Cosmetics Rule, 1945. The statements that are given in the monographs under the side heading "labeling" are not comprehensive.

19. Appendices: It contains general information. For e.g. The I.P. 1985 have the following appendix:

Appendix No.	Contents
Appendix No. 1	Apparatus for test and assay. E.g., Volumetric flask, thermometer etc.
Appendix No. 2	Biological tests and assays
Appendix No. 3	Chemical tests and assays
Appendix No. 4	Microbiological tests and assays
Appendix No. 5	Physical tests and determinations such as pH, melting point, etc.
Appendix No. 6	General Information

1.4 New Inclusion / Exclusion of Monograph

Due to decrease in the number of drugs in India, keeping in mind the medical advantages, there are inclusions or exclusions.

1. Storage and labeling included in the information section of monograph.

2. Structural formulae included.

3. Some titles have been changed to include more commonly accepted names in India. Example Hyoscine HBr for Scopolamine HBr.

4. Due to greater specificity of IR and UV tests in establishing identity, these are provided as alternative tests in addition to classical chemical tests.

5. HPLC introduced in addendum II of 1985 has been extended to many formulations that can be otherwise be analysed by more difficult or less accurate methods.

6. Qualitative tests have been replaced by quantitative tests for determination of particulate matter.

7. Bicarbonate deleted due to instability.

8. Design and statistical analysis of biological assay is extensively revised.

9. Veterinary monographs on vaccines such as infectious disease have been added.

10. Numbers of monographs have been upgraded. Example, acyclovir, alprazolam, captopril, mannitol, thiotepa, albendazole etc.

Question Bank

1. Define pharmaceutical chemistry?

2. Explain the various aspects of pharmaceutical chemistry.

3. Explain the importance of inorganic chemistry in pharmacy.

4. Explain about various pharmacopoeias.

5. Write the salient features of recent editions of Indian Pharmacopoeia.

6. Briefly explain about the storage conditions of drugs.

7. Describe the development of Pharmacopoeias.

8. Briefly explain the history of Indian Pharmacopoeia.

9. Write in brief the contents of Monograph.

10. Short note on monograph IP.

11. Explain the terms 'pharmacopoeia' and 'monograph'. Enlist different Pharmacopoeias and discuss salient features of monograph.

12. Discuss the storage conditions as detailed in I.P.

13. Describe briefly the content of a monograph?

14. Define monograph. Elaborate contents of monograph

15. Various identification tests as per IP.

✍ ✍ ✍

Chapter **2**...

Sources of Contamination in Pharmaceuticals and Methods to Control

Contents ...

2.1   Introduction

2.2   Sources of Impurities

2.3   Monograph

2.4   Limit Tests

    2.4.1   Limit Test for Chlorides

    2.4.2   Limit Test for Sulphates

    2.4.3   Limit Test for Iron

    2.4.4   Limit Test for Lead

    2.4.5   Limit Test for Heavy Metals

    2.4.6   Limit Test for Arsenic

    2.4.7   Limits of Insoluble and Soluble Matter

2.5   Qualitative Tests for Alkalis and Alkaline Earth Metals

•   Question Bank

2.1 Introduction

The purpose of drug substances or drug formulations (pharmaceuticals) is primarily for the well-being of humans. They cure patients of diseases, disorders or deficiencies. They cure due to their potency and therapeutic efficacy. However, these properties are also related to another important characteristic; and that is purity. Today a large number of drugs, chemicals and other substances are used in formulations. Keeping in mind the above fact as well as the prevelant global competition, it is, however, pertinent that pharmaceutical chemicals and formulations must maintain a very high degree of purity. A compound is said to be impure if it has foreign matter/impurities. These impurities affect its potency.

Although, it is almost impossible to attain 100% purity, technically as well as, cost wise, it is still possible to achieve a high degree of purity. Today's globalisation has increased competitiveness and awareness about quality of drugs and markets demand in general >99% purity.

Purity, though can be achieved through the process of purification, it is many a times economically less viable.

Alternatively, a reasonably acceptable purity can be achieved by controlling various sources or reasons that add to the impure nature of an active pharmaceutical ingredient, or drug as well as excipients used in pharmaceutical formulations. Pharmacopoeias have fixed the limit for these impurities.

2.2 Sources of Impurities

Effects of Impurities on Pharmaceuticals

1. Some impurities if present beyond certain tolerance limits can cause untoward side effects that can lead to unpleasant reactions. e.g., Heavy metals like Pb, Fe and As salts.

2. Some impurities which are otherwise harmless in nature and without any therapeutic effect, if present in considerable proportions dilute the active strength or potency of the drug substance. e.g, Na, K, Cl, SO_4, CO_3 salts.

3. Some impurities may be able to catalyse the degradation, thereby shortening the shelf life of the drug substance.

4. Some impurities by their chemical nature can interact with the drug substance to affect its purity and potency. Such impurities are said to be incompatible with the drug substance/s.

5. Some impurities by virtue of their unstable nature like hygroscopic nature, oxidisable nature etc., can bring about change in the physical properties like change in appearance, taste, odour, stability etc., of the drug substance causing technical difficulties in its use as well as formulation.

Impurities may enter or are formed in a drug substance during any of the following three stages;

1. During manufacturing.
2. During purification and processing.
3. During storage.

1. **During Manufacturing**

(a) **Raw Materials employed :** Impurities present in raw materials may be carried through the manufacturing process to contaminate the final product. Impurities such as As, Pb, heavy metals, chlorides associated with Na compounds, H_2SO_4 with $CuSO_4$ and HCl with $FeCl_3$ are some common examples. Likewise many elements accompany others in traces.

(b) **Reagents used in manufacturing process :** The quality and purity of reagents used for manufacturing the drug substances are very important. If reagents used in the manufacturing process contain some impurities these may find entry into the final product. For e.g. Sulphuric acid is used in many chemical processes. This acid often has lead present in it. Anions like Cl^- and SO_4^{-2} are common impurities in many substances because of the use of hydrochloric acid and sulphuric acid respectively in processing.

(c) **Solvents used in the manufacturing process :** The manufacturing processes may involve a single step or multiple steps (unit operations). Naturally, solvents play an important role next to the main reagents as most of the chemical reactions involved in these processes are solvent based. If proper quality/purity of solvents is not assured, they may add to the impurities. Solvents like toluene, n-butanol contain water as an azeotrope. Alcoholic solvents also may be contaminated with water and ethyl acetate can contain acetic acid in small amounts. Thus, quality of solvents needs to be assured and controlled.

(d) **Reaction vessels:** The reaction vessels employed in the manufacturing process may be metallic (cast iron, mild steel, stainless steel) or mild steel with glass lining. Nowadays, wooden or other metallic vessels are not used in pharma industry. Some solvents and reagents employed in the process may react with the metals of the reaction vessels, leading to their corrosion and passing traces of metal impurities into the solution, contaminating the final product. Similarly, glass vessels may leach traces of alkali into the solvent. Even if acids like HCl if by chance contain a small amount of fluoride, it can itch the glass lining and begin the metallic contamination. Lead antimony, bismuth etc. can crop up as impurities from the vessels.

(e) **Intermediate products in manufacturing process :** Some intermediates which are produced during the manufacture may be carried out through the final product as impurities. Intermediates are products of (i) incomplete conversion of reactants to final products or (ii) side or competing reactions or (iii) decomposition of products formed due to poor process control. In the manufacturing process of KI, the intermediate iodate is the main impurity. Similarly, sodium bromate is the impurity in NaBr.

(f) **Defects in manufacturing process :** Defects like imperfect mixing, non–adherence to optimum reaction conditions (proper temperature, pressure and pH) may lead to impurities. E.g., Improper heating (failing to achieve bright red temperatures) in process of manufacture of Zinc Oxide can lead to un oxidised metallic Zn as an impurity.

$$2Zn + O_2 \longrightarrow 2ZnO + Zn \text{ (impurity)}$$

(g) **Manufacturing hazards :** In industrial areas, the atmosphere is contaminated with dust particles (Al_2O_3, silica glass, carbon, gases like H_2S, SO_2, CO_2, CO etc.). During the manufacture of pharmaceutical products, these impurities may enter the final product. Accidental inclusion of dirt or glass or porcelain or silica or carbon or fibre particles due to poor manufacturing practices and facilities unable to check atmospheric and cross contaminations can lead to unwanted particulate matters in the product in many ways. These need to be checked and controlled. Wear and tear of machineries may shed metallic particles.

2. During Purification and Processing

Often if not properly controlled, impurities also get added during the purification processes, mainly through the purifying reagents, solvents or vessels used.

(a) Reagents used to remove other impurities : Sometimes some chemicals are added to remove or to precipitate another substance. This may be also give rise to source of impurity. For e.g. $BaCl_3$ is added to remove excess of sulphate in $AlCl_3$, hence $AlCl_3$ is likely to contain Ba as an impurity.

(b) Solvents used in process of purifications : Often the solvents used for purification can be sources of impurities. These solvents range from organic solvents to acids (organic as well as mineral) and of course water.

Water is the cheapest solvent and most widely used. Therefore it is known as universal solvent.

Types of water used are

(i) Tap water : It contains impurities of Na^+, Ca^{2+}, Mg^{2+}, CO_3^{2-}, SO_2^{-4} which when used appear as impurities in the final product.

(ii) Softened water : It contains Na^+ and Cl^- ions as impurities which when used may appear as impurities in the final product.

(iii) Demineralised water : Though it is free from all above inorganic ion- impurities it still contains organic impurities like salts of carboxylic acids, N and S etc.

(iv) Distilled water : Considered to be the best. It is pure water and is free from all inorganic and organic impurities but the cost of it's production is very high.

(c) Contamination due to vessels and equipment used for purification : During the purification processes, if the vessels are defective or not perfectly cleaned and dried they may add impurities like metallic ions, rust, glass particles, moisture etc.

The other equipment mainly the filters, centrifuges, dryers etc., also need to be clean and dry.

3. During Storage and Packaging

(a) Errors in the packaging or use of substandard packaging material : During the process of packaging or filling and sealing , whether applicable for solid dosage forms or liquid dosage forms or API , proper material which can ensure complete foolproof packaging without access to atmosphere and light will ensure the stability of the product. Thus, quality and strength of packaging material is very important.

E.g., if the aluminium foil for tablet strip or cap for a liquid formulation bottle is of substandard quality it can add to impurities. This may lead to recalls of entire batches from the market. This is very critical for parenteral formulations.

(b) Faulty packaging processes : Most of the pharmaceutical packaging processes are assembly lined automated process, generally involving pressing and sealing with heat. If the process parameters are not optimised or are tampered with, then it may lead to contaminations. E.g., Nowadays most of the parenteral products are in polymer containers using FFS (Form-Fill-Seal) processes which involve proper heating, filling, sealing and congealing cylces. Any changes in process parameters can be hazardous.

(c) Microbial Contamination : Microbial contaminations, mainly in the form of fungal and bacterial growth may be due to the result of improper storage conditions as well as faulty packaging. The products for parenteral administration and ophthalmic preparations have to undergo sterility tests.

2.3 Monograph

The pharmacopoeias of various countries e.g., I.P. B.P., Eur. P., U.S.P, Int. P., USSRP, J. P. prescribe set limits for purity of drug substances as the tolerance limits for various impurities for most of the drug substances. The corresponding information and values provided in the pharmacopoeias for drug substances is termed as Official Standards, and the drug substance for which it is described and obeys the requirements of the pharmacopoeia is termed as Official Substance. Thus, a drug is recognised as official vis-à-vis a pharmacopoeia, if it is included in it.

The pharmacopoeia takes cognizance of the purity, nature, methods and hazards of manufacture, precautions of storage and ultimately the conditions under which the product is to be used before fixing the permissible limits for any pharmaceutical substance official in it.

The pharmacopoeia enlists a battery of tests including visual description to assay or even storage conditions for any drug substance official in it. This is called the Mongraph.

A monograph generally includes :

- Description of the Drug or Finished Product
- Identification Tests
- Physical Constants
- Assay of Pharmaceutical Substances
- Assay of Principal Active Ingredients in Formulated Dosage Forms
- Limit Test
- Other specific tests
- Storage Conditions

Description: It is the information on the state, colour, odour, taste, nature (in case of solids – amorphous or crystalline), for any drug substance.

Identification Tests: Identification of a drug may be accomplished by a battery of tests ranging from physical tests to chemical tests.

The physical tests include determination of physical constants such as,

- melting point/boiling point,
- refractive index,

- weight per millilitre,
- specific optical rotation,
- light absorption,
- viscosity,
- specific surface area,
- swelling power,
- infra-red absorption, and
- The chromatographic tests like spot-tests by thin-layer chromatography (TLC) of pure drug *vs* the standard system.

Chemical tests used for identification are basically qualitative, confirming the presence of the substance under investigation.

Assay of Pharmaceutical Substances: An assay method should be specific for the substance or chemical species being examined. It is carried out by well defined general quantitative analysis based on specific reactions of one or more of the functional moieties present in a drug molecule.

Limit Tests: These are quantitative or semi-quantitative tests designed to identify or control small quantities of impurities. These tests should be specific and sensitive.

Other specific tests: These include sulphated ash, loss on drying, clarity and colour   of solution, presence of heavy metals and specific tests.

2.4 Limit Tests

Limit = A value or amount that is likely to be present in a substance.

Test = To examine or to investigate

Impurity = A foreign matter present in a compound

Definition

Limit test is defined as a quantitative or semi-quantitative test designed to identify and control small quantities of impurities which are likely to be present in the substance.

Importance of Limit Tests

To find out the harmful amount of impurities

To find out avoidable / unavoidable amount of impurities.

Types of Limit Tests

1. Comparison method
2. Quantitative determination
3. Test in which there is no visible reaction

General principle

1. If the sample is lighter (in colour/turbidity/opalescence) than the standard solution then it is within the pharmacopeial limit (accepted)

2. If the sample is darker/heavier than the standard solution then it is above the pharmacopeial limit (rejected).

3. **Specificity of a Limit Test :** A given limit test for a trace impurity should involve some selective reaction of the reagent with the trace impurity under consideration/ detection specifically characteristic only to it.

4. **Sensitivity of a Limit Test :** As most of the limit tests involve dilute solutions and results are based on concentration of the trace impurity, the results may take longer duration to become observable of appreciable. Thus, consideration of duration of test need to be of prime consideration in designing the limit test.

NESSLER Cylinder (IP appendix VII A127)

It is a clear glass cylinder with normal capacity of 50 ml, the overall height is about 15 cm, the external height to the 50 ml mark 11.0 to 12.4 cm, the thickness of the wall is around 1.0 to 1.5 mm and the thickness of the base is about 1.0 to 3.0mm. The external height to the 50 mark of cylinders used for the test must not differ by more than 1 mm.

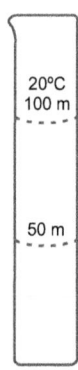

20°C
100 m
- - - -

50 m
- - - -

Fig. 2.1 : Nessler Cylinder

General Precautions

1. The liquid used must be clean and filtered if necessary.
2. The Nessler cylinder must be made of colourless glass and of the same inner diameter.
3. Detecting opalescence or colour development must be performed in daylight.
4. Comparison of turbidity, it should be done against a black background.
5. Comparison of colour it should be done against a white background.

2.4.1 Limit Test for Chlorides

Apparatus Required	**Chemicals Required**
Nessler cylinders	Dilute Nitric acid (10%)
Glass rod	Silver nitrate (5%)
Stand	Sodium chloride

Reaction

$$Cl^- + AgNO_3 \xrightarrow{\text{dil HNO}_3} AgCl\downarrow + NO_3^-$$

Principle

It is based upon the chemical reaction between silver nitrate and soluble chlorides in the presence of dilute nitric acid to give opalescence of silver chloride. The opalescence produced is compared with the standard solution. If the opalescence in the sample is less than the standard, it passes the test. If it is more than the standard, it fails the test.

Procedure

Take two 50 ml Nessler cylinders. Label one as "Test" and the other as "Standard".

Standard	Test
1. Place 1ml of 0.05845% w/v solution of NaCl in a Nessler cylinder.	1. Dissolve the specified quantity of the substance in distilled water and transfer to Nessler cylinder.
2. Add 10ml of dil. HNO$_3$.	2. Add 10ml of dil. HNO$_3$.
3. Dilute to 50ml with water and add 1 ml of silver nitrate solution.	3. Dilute to 50ml with water and add 1 ml of silver nitrate solution.
4. Stir immediately with a glass rod and allow to stand for 5 minutes.	4. Stir immediately with a glass rod and allow to stand for 5 minutes.
5. Observe the opalescence developed and compare with that of the sample.	5. Observe the opalescence developed and compare with that of the standard.

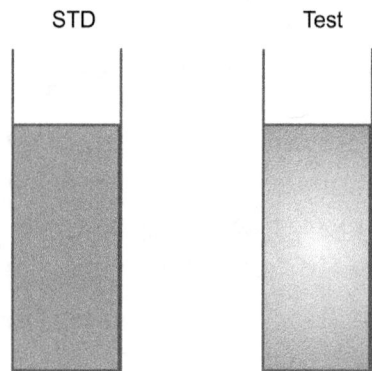

STD   Test

Fig 2.2 : The opalescence in STD is seen more than that of the Test; thus, the sample passes the limit test of chloride

2.4.2 Limit Test for Sulphates

| **Apparatus Required** | **Chemicals Required** |

Apparatus Required

Nessler cylinders

Glass rod

Stand

Chemicals Required

1. Dilute hydrochloric acid
2. 0.5 M Barium chloride : 122.1 g of $BaCl_2. 2H_2O$ dissolved in DW.
2. Barium sulphate reagent containing 0.5 M Barium chloride in 1000 ml of water. (*This is prepared as follows:*

   Mix 15ml of 0.5M $BaCl_2$, 55ml of water and 20ml of sulphate free alcohol. Add 5 ml of 0.0181% w/v potassium sulphate. Dilute to 10ml with water and mix.)

Reaction

$$SO_4^{2-} + BaCl_2 \xrightarrow{\text{dil } H_2SO_4} BaSO_4\downarrow + 2Cl^-$$

Principle

It is based upon the chemical reaction between barium chloride and soluble sulphate in the presence of dilute hydrochloric acid. The turbidity produced is compared with the standard solution. Barium chloride reagent contains barium chloride, sulphate – free alcohol and small quantity of potassium sulphate. The inclusion of the small quantity of potassium sulphate in the reagent increases the sensitivity of the test. Alcohol prevents super saturation and a more uniform turbidity develops. If the turbidity produced in the test is more intense than the standard turbidity, then the drug fails the test ,otherwise, it passes the test.

Procedure

Take two 50 ml Nessler Cylinders. Label one as "Test" and the other as "Standard".

Standard	**Test**
1. Place 1ml of 0.1089% w/v solution of K_2SO_4 in a Nessler cylinder.	1. Dissolve the specified quantity of the substance in distilled water and transfer to Nessler cylinder.
2. Add 2 ml of dil. HCl.	2. Add 2 ml of dil. HCl.
3. Dilute to 45ml with water and add 5 ml of barium sulphate reagent reagent.	3. Dilute to 45ml with water and add 5 ml of barium sulphate reagent.
4. Stir immediately with a glass rod and allow to stand for 5 minutes.	4. Stir immediately with a glass rod and allow to stand for 5 minutes.
5. Observe the turbidity developed and compare with that of the sample.	5. Observe the turbidity developed and compare with that of the standard.

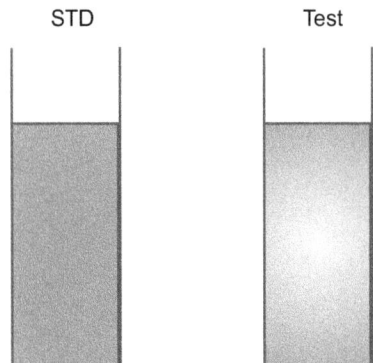

STD   Test

Fig 2.3: The turbidity in STD is seen less than that of the Test; thus, the sample fails the limit test of chloride

2.4.3 Limit Test for Iron

Apparatus Required   **Chemicals Required**

Nessler cylinders

Glass rod

Stand

1. **STD Iron solution :** Ferric ammonium sulphate (1.726 g) dissolved in 10 ml of 0.1 N H_2SO_4 and sufficient water to produce 1000 ml.
2. Sulphuric acid (0. 1 N) : 10.0 ml.
3. Iron-free citric acid solution (20% w/v) : 2.0 ml.
4. Thioglycollic acid : 0.1 ml.
5. Iron-free ammonia solution : 20 ml.

Reaction

$$Fe^{2+} + \underset{\underset{\text{Thioglycolic acid}}{COOH}}{\overset{CH_2SH}{|}} \longrightarrow \underset{\underset{\text{ferrous thioglycolate}}{COOH \quad HSH_2C}}{\overset{CH_2SH \qquad OOC}{\diagdown Fe \diagup}} + 2H^+$$

Principle

The test depends upon the reaction between ferrous iron and thioglycollic acid in the presence of ammonia. A pale pink to deep reddish purple colour is produced. Ferric iron is reduced to ferrous iron by the thioglycollic acid and the compound produced is ferrous thioglycollate. Citric acid forms a soluble complex with iron and prevents its precipitation by ammonia as ferrous hydroxide. Ferrous thioglycollate is colourless in neutral or acid solutions. The colour develops only in the presence of alkali. It is stable in the absence of air but fades when exposed to air due to oxidation to the ferric compound. Therefore, the colours should be compared immediately after the time allowed for full development of colour is over.

Procedure

Take two 50 ml Nessler Cylinders. Label one as "Test" and the other as 'Standard'.

Standard	Test
1. Dilute 2 ml of standard Iron solution with 20ml of water in a Nessler cylinder.	1. Dissolve the specified quantity of the substance in distilled water and transfer to Nessler cylinder.
2. Add 2ml of 20% w/v solution of iron – free citric acid and 0.1 ml of thioglycollic acid and mix.	2. Add 2ml of 20% w/v solution of iron – free citric acid and 0.1 ml of thioglycollic acid and mix.
3. Make alkaline with iron-free ammonia solution.	3. Make alkaline with iron-free ammonia solution.
4. Dilute to 50 ml with water.	4. Dilute to 50 ml with water.
5. Observe the intensity of the purple colour developed by viewing vertically and compare with that of the sample.	5. Observe the intensity of the purple colour developed by viewing vertically and compare with that of the standard.

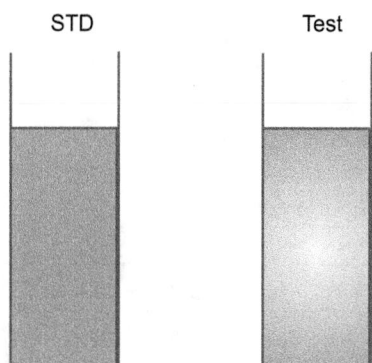

Fig. 2.4 : The intensity of the colour in STD is seen less than that of the Test; thus, the sample fails the limit test of iron

2.4.4 Limit Test for Lead

Lead is one of the most undesirable impurities and enters through storage containers like bottle caps, as well as some apparatus.

It has two different variants in of limit tests. The first one is more specific for lead.

TEST-1 : Reaction with Dithizone : This test is official in IP and USP.

TEST-2 : It is described under Limit Test for Heavy Metals after this limit test.

Reaction

$$Pb^{++} + 2.\ S = \begin{matrix} NHNH\text{-}C_6H_5 \\ NHNH\text{-}C_6H_5 \end{matrix} \xrightarrow{\ OH-\ }$$

Dithizone

Lead-Dithizone complex

Principle

Its limit test is based upon the chemical reaction between lead and diphenylthio-carbazone (dithizone) in alkaline solution to form lead dithizone, which is red in colour. (Dithizone itself is green in colour and the lead dithizone formed is violet in colour. Thus, the net resultant colour of the solution becomes red). The lead present in the impurity is first extracted using the dithizone extraction solution. To avoid interference by other metals and make the pH optimum, reagents like ammonium citrate, KCN and $NH_2OH.HCl$ are employed. Phenol red is used as an indicator to develop colour at the end of the process.

Procedure

Take two 50 ml Nessler Cylinders. Label one as "Test" and the other as 'Standard'.

Standard	Test
1. A standard lead solution (1 ppm Pb) is prepared equivalent to the amount of lead permitted in the sample under examination.	1. A known quantity of sample solution is transferred in a separating funnel.
2. Add 6ml of ammonium citrate.	2. Add 6ml of ammonium citrate.
3. Add 2 ml of potassium cyanide and 2 ml of hydroxylamine hydrochloride.	3. Add 2 ml of potassium cyanide and 2 ml of hydroxylamine hydrochloride.
4. Make solution alkaline by adding ammonia solution.	4. Make solution alkaline by adding ammonia solution.
5. Extract with 5 ml of dithizone in chloroform solution, until it becomes green.	5. Extract with 5 ml of dithizone in chloroform solution, until it becomes green.
6. Dithizone extracts are shaken for 30 mins with 30 ml of nitric acid and the chloroform layer is discarded.	6. Dithizone extracts are shaken for 30 mins with 30 ml of nitric acid and the chloroform layer is discarded.

... (Contd.)

Standard	Test
7. To the acid solution add 5 ml of standard dithizone solution.	7. To the acid solution add 5 ml of standard dithizone solution.
8. Add 4 ml of ammonium cyanide.	8. Add 4 ml of ammonium cyanide.
9. Shake for 30 mins.	9. Shake for 30 mins.
10. Observe the colour.	10. Observe the colour.

Observation

The colour comparison of Standard and Test solutions is done to decide whether sample passes or fails.

2.4.5 Limit Test for Heavy Metals

It is a limit test of the quantity of heavy metals contained as impurities in drugs. The heavy metals are the metallic inclusions that are darkened with sodium sulfide(TS) in acidic solution or hydrogen sulphide saturated solution,as their quantity is expressed in terms of the quantity of lead (Pb).

In each monograph, the permissible limit for heavy metals (as Pb) is described in terms of ppm in parentheses.

Apparatus Required

Nessler cylinders

Glass rod

Stand

Chemicals Required

1. Dilute CH_3COOH(10% v/v)
2. Dilute Ammonia (10% v/v)
3. Hydrogen sulphide solution (Saturated solution of H_2S). (or sodium sulphide solution)
4. Standard lead solution (10 ml of the lead nitrate stock solution diluted to 100 ml with water. (20 ppm of lead).
5. Lead nitrate stock solution: Dissolve 0.1598 gm of lead nitrate in 100 ml of water, add 1 ml of con HNO_3 and dilute to 1000 ml with water.

Reaction

$$Pb(NO_3)_2 \ (Pb^+) + H_2S \rightarrow PbS\downarrow + 2HNO_3$$
$$PbCl_2 + Na_2S \rightarrow PbS\downarrow + 2NaCl$$

Principle

It is based on the reaction between the solution of heavy metals and a saturated solution of hydrogen sulphide. In acidic media, it produces reddish / black colour with hydrogen sulphide which is compared with standard lead nitrate solution.

Procedure

Take two 50 ml Nessler cylinders. Label one as "Test" and the other as 'Standard'.

Standard	Test
1. 2 ml of standard lead solution is taken in a Nessler cylinder and diluted to 25 ml with water.	1. Dissolve the specified quantity of the substance in distilled water diluted to 25 ml with water and transfer to Nessler cylinder.
2. Adjust the pH to 3-4 by dil. acetic acid or dil. ammonia solution.	2. Adjust the pH to 3-4 by dil. acetic acid or dil. ammonia solution.
3. Dilute further to 35 ml with water.	3. Dilute further to 35 ml with water
4. Add 10 ml of freshly prepared H_2S solution.	4. Add 10 ml of freshly prepared H_2S solution.
5. Dilute to 50ml with water.	5. Dilute to 50ml with water.
6. Mix and allow to stand for five minutes.	6. Mix and allow to stand for five minutes.
7. Observe the quantity of the black ppt of lead sulphide formed and compare with that of the standard.	7. Observe the quantity of the black ppt of lead sulphide formed and compare with that of the standard.

STD   Test

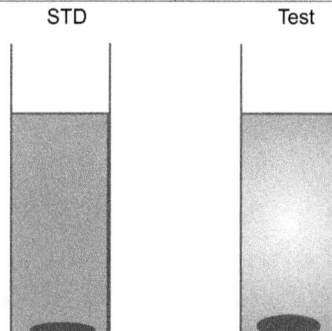

Fig 2.5 : The quantity of the black ppt of lead sulphide in STD is seen less than that of the Test. Thus, the sample fails the limit test of heavy metals.

2.4.6 Limit Test for Arsenic

Apparatus Required

Arsenic limit test apparatus;

$HgCl_2$—paper :smooth white filter paper (having thickness not less than 25 mm), soaked in a saturated solution of $HgCl_2$, pressed to get rid of excess of solution and dried at about 60°C in the dark.

Chemicals Required

Lead acetate solution: 10.0% w/v soln. of $PbAc_2$ in

CO_2 – free water ;

KI (AsT), 1.0 g ;

Zn (AsT) : l0.0 g ;

Dilute Arsenic solution (AST);

Standard stains, Test Solutions—are prepared according to the Indian Pharmacopoeia 1996.

Reaction

Various chemical reactions involved may be expressed by the following equations -

$$Zn + 2HCl \rightarrow ZnCl_2 + 2(H)$$
$$2As + 6(H) \rightarrow 2AsH_3 \uparrow$$
$$HgCl_2 + AsH_3 \rightarrow HgCl_2. AsH_3$$
Yellow complex

Principle

The principle is based on **Gutzeit Test** wherein, all arsenic present is duly converted into arsine gas (AsH_3) by subjecting it to reduction with zinc and hydrochloric acid. Further, it depends upon the fact that when arsine in presence of a reducing agent like KI, comes into contact with dry paper permeated with mercuric (Hg^{2+})chloride it produces a yellow stain, the intensity of which is directly proportional to the quantity of arsenic present. It requires a special apparatus.

Procedure

Take two 50 ml of Arsenic LT apparatus bottles. Label one as "Test" and the other as "Standard".

Standard	Test
1. A known amount of dilute arsenic solution is kept in the wide mouthed bottle of the apparatus.	1. Test Solution: Dissolving specific amount of sample in water and stannate HCl (As free) and kept in the wide mouthed bottle of the apparatus.
2. To this solution 1 gm of KI, 5 ml of stannous chloride and 10 gm of zinc is added (all these reagents should be As free.)	2. To this solution 1 gm of KI, 5 ml of stannous chloride and 10 gm of zinc is added (all these reagents should be As free.)
3. Keep the solution aside for 40 min.	3. Keep the solution aside for 40 min.
4. Compare the stain obtained on the mercuric chloride paper with that in the apparatus containing test solution.	4. Compare the stain obtained on the mercuric chloride paper with that in the apparatus containing standard solution.

Notes

Arsenic Limit Test Apparatus

1. A 120 ml capacity, wide-mouthed bottle fitted with a rubber bung through which passes a glass tube of approx. 20 cm and 6-8 mm diameter is used. One end of this tube is constricted like that of a pipette with 1 mm diameter having a hole of 2 mm diameter.

2. When the bung is inserted in the bottle containing 70 ml of liquid, the constricted end of the tube should be above the surface of the liquid, and the hole in the side is below the bottom of the bung.

3. The upper end of the tube is cut off square, and is either slightly rounded or ground smooth.

4. The rubber bungs (about 25 mm × 25 mm), each with a hole bored centrally and through, exactly 6.5 mm in diameter, are fitted with a rubber band or spring clip for holding them tightly in place.

5. The glass tube is lightly packed with cotton wool, previously moistened with lead acetate solution and dried, so that the upper surface of the cotton wool is not less than 25 mm below the top of the tube.

6. The upper end of the tube is then inserted into the narrow end of one of the pair of rubber bungs, to a depth of l0 mm (the tube must have a rounded-off end).

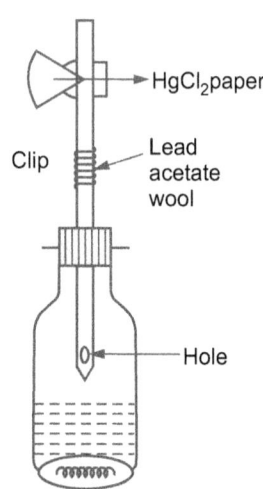

Figure 2.6: Apparatus for Limit Test of Arsenic

7. A piece of mercuric chloride paper is placed flat on the top of the bung and the other bung placed over it and secured by means of the spring clip in such a manner that the holes of the two bungs meet to form a true tube 6.5 mm diameter interrupted by a diaphragm of mercuric chloride paper.

2.4.7 Limits of Insoluble and Soluble Matter

The pharmacopoeias prescribe permissible limits of insoluble (inorganic) and soluble matters in official drug substances. Some of the examples are as follows-

Limits of Insoluble Matter

1. **Boric acid :** No alcohol insoluble substances /matter tolerated
2. **Phenobarbitone sodium:** Alcohol insoluble substances /matter tolerated NMT 0.3%, that should be non-acidic in nature
3. **Crystal violet:** Insoluble inorganic salts NMT 1.0%
4. Similarly many substances are tested for clarity of their aqueous solutions to limit water insoluble substances.

Limits of Soluble Matter

In order to limit certain specific impurities generally present in official drug substances the pharmacopoeias prescribe permissible limits of soluble impurities also.

1. Barium sulphate (X-Ray grade): The sample is boiled and digested with dil HCl and filtered and evaporated and reconstituted with DW to check if any water soluble matter is present. Water soluble salts of barium are toxic and not permissible.

2. On similar lines light kaolin and purified talc are tested using dil HCl or dil H_2SO_4. The limits for the former is NMT 0.5% and later is NMT 250 ppm.

Non-Volatile Matter, Residue on Ignition and Ash Values

Limits of Non-Volatile Matter : To distinguish between impurities of organic and inorganic origins as well as small to polymeric molecular structures, pharmacopoeias prescribe permissible limits under two different categories -

- Readily Volatile Matter of organic origins like alcohols, alkanes, alkenes, ethers, phenols etc., as well as those of inorganic origins like ammonia, hydrogen peroxide, water etc.

- Substances which are volatile on strong ignition such as hard and soft paraffins, anhydrous lanolin, etc.

Residue on Ignition : Pharmacopoeias prescribe permissible limits also under two different categories

- Substances which are totally volatile on ignition and don't leave any residue. E.g., Mercury (Hg)

- Substances which decompose and leave a residue of definite composition. E.g., Basic ZnO.

Ash Values: Ash values indicate the extent of inorganic matter in a drug substance in form of a residue when ignited at specific temperatures. They are of 4 types-

1. **Total Ash or Ash Value :** Indicates the extent of inorganic and extraneous matters. Generally the drug sample is ignited to ~450°C in a silica dish till free from carbon.

2. **Acid insoluble Ash :** The total ash comprises of inorganic materials as well as soil particles in case of drugs from herbal origin. To differentiate between these two impurities, a treatment of acid is given to the total ash and the matter remaining insoluble in acid is estimated.

3. **Sulfated Ash :** The sample is ignited on a silica crucible at ~650°C in presence of a small amount 1M sulphuric acid, till all black ash particles are cooled and thereafter neutralised and estimated.

4. **Water soluble Ash :** The total ash is boiled with DM water and residual loss is estimated.

2.5 Qualitative Tests for Alkali and Alkaline Earth Metals

1. **Barium :** Presence of barium is confirmed by addition of dilute sulphuric acid to the test solution, which should yield precipitate of barium sulphate.

2. **Calcium :** Presence of calcium is confirmed by addition of dilute ammonium oxalate to the ethanolictest solution, which should yield precipitate of calcium oxalate.

3. **Magnesium :** Confirmed by formation of magnesium 8-hydroxyquinoline (oxine) complex. Alternately, if calcium is present it is to be removed as calcium oxalate, and then magnesium is precipitated as sulphate.

4. **Aluminium :** Confirmed by formation of aluminium 8-hydroxyquinoline (oxine) complex and measurement of its fluorescence.

Question Bank

1. Give principle involved in limit test for Iron as per I.P and describe it.
2. Write in detail raw materials as source of impurity.
3. Enlist various sources of impurities. Discuss manufacturing hazards in detail.
4. Write in detail Limit Test of Arsenic with its modifications.
5. Write specifications of Nessler cylinder as per Pharmacopoeia.
6. Write the modifications of limit test of Lead.
7. Give the role of –
   (i) Lead acetate cotton plug in limit test of Arsenic.
   (ii) Thioglycolic acid in limit test of Iron.
8. Discuss limit test of chloride for potassium permanganate.
9. Effect of impurities on properties of substances.
10. Why is the tube packed with dried cotton wool impregnated with lead acetate solution while carrying out limit test for arsenic?
11. Write the principle involved in limit test for lead.
12. Enlist sources of impurities in pharmaceutical substances and explain their effects on pharmaceutical substances.
13. Describe the limit test for Iron.
14. Discuss various sources of impurities in pharmaceutical substances.
15. Explain ash value and its significance.
16. Why stannated hydrochloric acid is used in limit test for arsenic.
17. Discuss the limit test for sulphate.
18. Elaborate various tests for purities
19. Explain the principle involved in the limit test for Lead I.P.
20. Illustrate the sources of impurities in pharmaceutical substances.
21. Explain he types of Impurities.
22. What is the effect of impurities on the quality of pharmaceuticals ? Explain.
23. Explain control of impurities.
24. Describe briefly the impurities getting added during the storage of pharmacopoeial substances.
25. Explain the importance of impurity for pharmacopoeial substances.
26. Write a brief essay on sources of impurity in pharmaceuticals.

Chapter 3...

Water

Contents ...

3.1 Introduction

3.2 Water as Universal Pharmaceutical Vehicle

3.3 Properties of Water

3.4 Hardness of Water

   3.4.1 Sources of Hardness

   3.4.2 Methods to Remove Temporary Hardness of Water

   3.4.3 Methods of Remove Permanent Hardness of Water

3.5 Different Official Waters

3.6 Official Tests for Water

• Question Bank

3.1 Introduction

Water is vital for life on earth. Pure water is colourless, odourless and tasteless. Water has the capacity to dissolve a variety of substances, is naturally available and is the cheapest solvent; hence is called as **"universal solvent"**. It covers about 70% of the earth's surface.

Water is life for all living beings on earth. It means that, wherever water goes, either through the air, the ground, or through our bodies, it takes along valuable chemicals, minerals and nutrients. Water is an excellent solvent due to its chemical composition and physical attributes. The polar nature of water molecule allows it to become attracted to different types of molecules to dissolve other compounds into it. At the molecular level, salt dissolves in water due to electrical changes.

3.2 Water as Universal Pharmaceutical Vehicle

In the pharmaceutical industry, water is most commonly and widely used as a vehicle not only in different formulations but, also as a cleansing agent.

Purified water used in pharma industry is usually produced *in-situ* from local potable water. If hard water containing calcium, magnesium and iron salts is used for preparing pharmaceutical formulations like, syrups, suspensions, ointments, injections etc., it may produce certain undesirable effects, which could be harmful to human beings or animals.

Different grades of water are required depending on the route of administration of the pharmaceutical products, *viz.,*

- Purified water
- Water for injection
- Sterile water for injection
- Bacteriostatic water for injection
- Water for thermodialysis
- Sterile water for inhalations
- Distilled water
- Deionised water
- Ammonia free water
- Carbon dioxide free water
- Nitrate free water.

3.3 Properties of Water

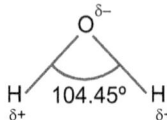

Fig. 3.1 : Molecular structure of water

- Water is the only natural substance existing in all three common states of matter as liquid, solid and gaseous state in the nature with molecular formula H_2O.
- At room temperature, it is a colourless, odourless and tasteless liquid, it freezes at 0°C to solid form ice and when heated to 100°C, it is converted into gaseous form (steam).
- The attraction between the most electronegative oxygen atom and electropositive hydrogen atom is known as **"Hydrogen Bonding"**. The molecules of water are constantly moving in relation to each other and the hydrogen bonds are continually breaking and forming at timescales faster than 200 femto seconds.
- Water has a very high specific heat capacity as well as heat of vaporisation.
- The density of water is approx. 1 gm per cubic centimetre. Ice is less dense than water, hence it floats in liquid water.
- Water is miscible with many liquids forming a single homogeneous liquid (hydrophilic-water loving). Water is immiscible with most oils (hydrophobic-water hating). As a gas, water vapour is completely miscible with air.
- An important feature of water is its polar nature.
- Water exhibits capillary action where by water rises into a narrow tube against the force of gravity.

Chemical Properties of Water

1. **Amphoteric nature of water :** It has the ability to act as either an acid or a base in chemical reactions.

Example : When water receives H^+ ion from HCl forming H_3O^+ hydronium ion, it acts as a base.

$$HCl \text{ (acid)} + H_2O \text{ (base)} \rightleftharpoons H_3O^+ + Cl^-$$

In the reaction with ammonia, NH_3, water donates H^+ ion and thus, acts as an acid.

$$NH_3 \text{ (base)} + H_2O \text{ (acid)} \rightleftharpoons NH_4^+ + OH^-$$

2. **Solvent property :** Water acts as an universal solvent. It is of great importance as a solvent in various pharmaceutical preparations.

3. **Redox property :** Water acts as an oxidising agent in reactions.

$$2Na + 2H_2O \longrightarrow 2NaOH + H_2\uparrow$$

Water is capable of acting as a reducing agent in some cases like with fluorine.

$$2H_2O + 2F_2 \longrightarrow 2H_2F_2 + O_2\uparrow$$

3.4 Hardness of Water

The amount of dissolved calcium and magnesium in water determines its "hardness". The degree of hardness becomes greater as the calcium and magnesium content increases. The hardness of water may be permanent or temporary. Hard water interferes with almost every cleaning task from bathing to personal grooming and laundering to dish washing. Hair becomes dull and sticky, dishes and glasses may be spotted when dry, filming develops on bathtubs, sinks, showers etc. and deposits develop in pipes which may reduce the water flow due to the use of hard water. Soap used in hard water combines with the minerals to form a sticky soap cud. Continuous laundering in hard water can shorten the life of clothes.

The National Academy of Sciences, United States of America, states that hard water contributes a small amount towards human dietary needs of calcium and magnesium. The hardness of water is determined as milligram per litre (mg/l) or parts per million (ppm). The water hardness can be classified as follows

Classification	mg/l or ppm
Soft water	0 – 17.1
Slightly hard water	17.1 – 60
Moderately hard water	60 – 120
Hard water	120 – 180
Very hard water	180 and above

3.4.1 Sources of Hardness

(a) Temporary hardness

(b) Permanent hardness

The temporary hardness of water is caused by the presence of dissolved bicarbonate minerals; $Ca(HCO_3)_2$ and $Mg(HCO_3)_3$.

Temporary hardness of water is due to rain water passing over rocks containing carbonate ions.

$$H_2O(l) + CO_2(g) + CaCO_3(s) \longrightarrow Ca(HCO_3)_2 \text{ (aq)}$$
$$H_2O(l) + CO_2(g) + MgCO_3(s) \longrightarrow Mg(HCO_3)_2 \text{ (aq)}$$

The temporary hardness can be reduced by boiling the water, which precipitates calcium carbonate out of the solution and makes water softer upon cooling. The lime softening process is also used to remove temporary hardness.

Permanent hardness of water is caused by presence of calcium sulphate ($CaSO_4$) and magnesium sulphate ($MgSO_4$). The permanent hardness of water is formed as water passes over rocks containing sulphate ions.

$$\text{Water} + CaSO_4(s) \longrightarrow Ca^{2+} + SO_4^{2-}$$
$$\text{(aq)} \quad \text{(aq)}$$
$$\text{Water} + MgSO_4(s) \longrightarrow Mg^{2+} + SO_4^{2-}$$
$$\text{(aq)} \quad \text{(aq)}$$

It cannot be removed by boiling but, can be removed by using water softners, ion exchange resins, distillation and washing with soda.

3.4.2 Methods to Remove Temporary Hardness of Water

There are 7 methods for softening of temporary hard water.

1. Boiling : When water boils at 100°C, the soluble bicarbonates are converted into insoluble bicarbonates as most of the CO_2 is removed. The insoluble bicarbonates sediment on cooling and are filtered out to get soft water. This method is not suitable for large volumes of temporary hard water.

$$Ca(HCO_3)_2 \xrightarrow{100°C} CaCO_3 \downarrow + H_2O + CO_2 \uparrow$$

2. Clark's Process (Addition of Slaked Lime) : In Clark's process, $Ca(OH)_2$, slaked lime is added to temporary hard water. Insoluble calcium carbonate precipitates out and the water becomes soft.

$$Ca(HCO_3)_2 + Ca(OH)_2 \longrightarrow 2CaCO_3 + 2H_2O$$
$$\text{Slaked lime} \qquad \text{Insoluble calcium carbonate}$$

The addition of too much slaked lime will impart permanent hardness to water, so care must be taken while adding slaked lime.

3. Addition of Washing Soda : This is a familiar method of softening temporary hard water used for household purposes. Calcium and magnesium ions present in hard water react with sodium carbonate to produce insoluble carbonates. It is inexpensive and easy to use.

$$CaSO_4 + Na_2CO_3 \longrightarrow CaCO_3\downarrow + Na_2SO_4$$
$$MgCl_2 + Na_2CO_3 \longrightarrow MgCO_3\downarrow + 2NaCl$$

4. Addition of Ammonia : Ammonia reacts with calcium bicarbonate to form insoluble calcium carbonate salt and soluble ammonium carbonate.

$$Ca(HCO_3)_2 + 2NH_3 \longrightarrow CaCO_3\downarrow + (NH_4)_2CO_3$$

5. Calgon Process : Calgon is a trade name of a complex salt, sodium hexametaphosphate $(NaPO_3)_6$. The addition of calgon to hard water causes the calcium and magnesium ions of hard water to displace sodium ions from the anion of calgon.

$$Ca^{2+} + Na_4P_6O_{18}^{2-} \longrightarrow 2Na^+ + CaNa_2P_6O_{18}^{2-}$$

Hard water Anion of   Goes into solution
          calgon

The water is softened and sodium ions are released into the water.

6. Ion Exchange Process (Permutit Process) : Permutit or sodium aluminium silicate is a complex chemical compound, which occurs as a natural mineral called **zeolite.** The process is based on an ion exchange reaction for softening water.

The slow stream of hard water is passed through zeolites. The calcium and magnesium ions present in hard water are exchanged with sodium ions in the permutit. The outgoing water contains sodium salt, which does not cause hardness.

$$CaCl_2 + 2Na^+ (Al\text{-silicate}) \longrightarrow Ca(Al\text{-silicate})_2 + 2NaCl$$
In hard water   Permutit

$$MgSO_4 + 2Na^+ (Al\text{-silicate}) \longrightarrow Mg(Al\text{-silicate})_2 + Na_2SO_4$$
In hard water   Permutit

7. Using Ion Exchange Resins : (Demineralised water or deionised water)

All the earlier methods leave some chemicals in the water, although water may be 'softened'. The development of commercial resinous ion exchangers in the year 1935, made possible the removal of both cations and anions from water. The removal of salts from water by this process consists of two steps.

Acid resins exchange their H^+ ions with other cations such as Ca^{2+}, Mg^{2+} etc. present in hard water. Acid resins are therefore known as base-exchange resins.

$$2RCOO^- + Ca^{2+} \longrightarrow (RCOO^-)_2 Ca + 2H^+$$
Acid resin   from hard water

Basic resins exchange their OH^- with other anions such as HCO_3^-, Cl^- SO_4^{2-}, present in hard water.

Basic resins, therefore also known as acid exchange resins.

$$RNH_3^+ \, OH^- + Cl^- \longrightarrow RNH_3^+ \, Cl + H^+$$

Basic resin   from water

3.4.3 Methods to Remove Permanent Hardness of Water

There are 4 different methods to treat permanent hard water as described below –

1. Using Soluble Alkali Carbonates : The addition of Na_2CO_3 or washing soda in permanent hard water precipitates calcium and magnesium present in it.

$$CaSO_4 + Na_2CO_3 \longrightarrow CaCO_3\downarrow + Na_2SO_4$$
$$MgSO_4 + Na_2CO_3 \longrightarrow MgCO_3\downarrow + Na_2SO_4$$

2. Chelation by Polyphosphate : In this method, metaphosphate polymers like sodium metaphosphate $(NaPO_3)_n$ or Graham's salt is used to remove permanent hardness of water. These salts form the soluble chelates with divalent cations like Ca^{2+}, Mg^{2+} or Fe^{2+}.

3. Zeolite Process : The method described in the softening of temporary hard water is used for softening permanent hard water.

$$Na_2(Zeol) + CaSO_4 \longrightarrow Ca(Zeol) + Na_2SO_4$$

4. Use of Ion Exchange Resin : The resinous ion-exchangers soften permanent hard water. The removal of $CaSO_4$ from permanent hard water is carried out in two steps as given below :

Step I : $2H \, (Resin) + CaSO_4 \longrightarrow Ca(Resin)_2 + H_2SO_4$

Step II : $2 \, (Resin) - NH_2 + H_2SO_4 \longrightarrow [(Resin) \, NH_3^+]_2 \cdot SO_4^{2-}$

3.5 Different Official Waters

The United States Pharmacoepia (USP) has 5 different types of water used in pharmaceutical industry for formulation of drugs.

1. Water
2. Purified water
3. Water for injection
4. Bacteriostatic water for injection
5. Sterile water for injection.

The above mentioned official water types should meet the purity requirements as per USP.

1. Water (USP)

- It is a clear, colourless and odourless liquid.
- It has pH in the range of 5 - 8.
- It should not contain any oxidisable substances.
- The total solid contents should not be more than 1000 ppm.

- It is free from bacteria.
- It is used to make different pharmaceutical formulations *viz.,* solutions, tinctures and extracts.

2. **Purified Water (USP)**
   - It is prepared by simple distillation or by ion exchange treatment from potable water.
   - It is clear, colourless and odourless liquid.
   - It is not intended for parentral administration.
   - Its pH is in the range of 5 - 7.
   - The pink colour of $KMnO_4$ remains faintly pink when 0.1 ml of 0.1 N $KMnO_4$ solution is added to 100 ml of purified water.
   - The total solid contents should not be more than 10 ppm.
   - The limit of total viable aerobic contaminants is 100 micro-organisms per ml.
   - Purified water is used for all tests and assays performed in pharmaceutical analysis.

3. **Water for Injection (USP)**
   - It is pyrogen free, purified water. Pyrogens are bacterial enxotoxins produced by micro-organisms which elevate normal body temperature.
   - It is used as a vehicle for the preparation of pharmaceutical parentral solutions.
   - It contains no added substances.
   - It is obtained by distilling potable water or purified water.
   - It has pH range of 5 - 7.

4. **Bacteriostatic Water for Injection (USP)**
   - It is a sterile form of water for injection with one or more suitable antimicrobial preservatives.
   - Benzyl alcohol is a common bacteriostatic agent used as preservative in bacteriostatic water for injection.
   - It does have specifications for antimicrobial agents, pyrogens and sterility.
   - It has pH range of 4.5 - 7.0.
   - It is stored in a single dose or multiple dose containers, preferably of Type I or Type II glass, not larger than 30 ml size.
   - The antimicrobial agents (s), name and concentration must be mentioned on the label.
   - This type of water is developed to dissolve drugs intended to be delivered through parentral route of administration by intramuscular (IM) injection.
   - This water is not used for intravenous (IV) route of administration due to presence of bacteriostatic agents.

5. **Sterile Water for Injection (USP)**
   - It is sterile, pyrogen free water with no added antimicrobial agents.
   - This water is most difficult to prepare.
   - It has pH in the range of 5 - 7.

- It may be stored in a single dose container of Type I or Type II glass.
- It is used for the extemporaneous compounding of parentrals for either IV or IM injection.

3.6 Official Tests for Water

1. **pH :** It should be between 4.5 - 7.0. The pH of water below 4.0 and above 9.0 is not allowed for use in pharmaceutical preparations.
2. **Clarity and colour :** All types of water should be clear, colourless and practically free from suspended particles.
3. **Heavy metals :** Not more than 0.1 ppm.
4. **Residue on evaporation :** The residue weight shall not be more than 1 mg.
5. **Bacterial endotoxins :** The limit of bacterial endotoxins shall be less than 0.25 IU/ml. This test is applicable to water for injection, sterile water for injection and bacteriostatic water for injection.
6. **Oxidisable substances :** To 100 ml of water, 10 ml of 1 M sulphuric acid and 0.1 ml of 0.02 M $KMnO_4$ solution are added and boiled for 5 minutes, the solution that remains faintly pink passes the test for oxidisable substances.
7. **Sterility test :** Applicable for waters used for parentral use.
8. **Test for pyrogen :** This test is applicable for water intended for preparation parentral preparations.

Question Bank

1. Comment on water as a universal solvent.
2. Describe different physical and chemical properties of water.
3. Define hardness of water. Discuss various methods to remove hardness of temporary and permanent hard water.
4. Describe various official waters.
5. Discuss different official tests of water.
6. Write a note on the following
   (a) Water as a pharmaceutical vehicle.
   (b) Hardness of water.
   (c) Clark's lime process.
   (d) Ion-exchange resin method.
   (e) Water for injection.
   (f) Sterile water for injection (USP).
   (g) Quality control tests of water.
   (h) Methods of softening temporary hard water.
   (i) Methods of softening permanent hard water.
7. State the differences between hard water and soft water.
8. Make a chart or table for different official waters, and compare them.

Chapter 4...

Gastrointestinal Agents

Contents ...

4.1 Introduction
4.2 Acidifying Agents
    4.2.1 Dilute Hydrochloric Acid I.P.
4.3 Antacids
    4.3.1 Combination Antacids
4.4 Protectives and Adsorbents
4.5 Saline Cathartics
• Question Bank

4.1 Introduction

The Gastro-Intestinal Tract (G.I.T.) is one of the important body systems comprising of many organs. These include, the oral cavity of the mouth, oesophagus, stomach, small intestine (duodenum, jejunum, and ileum), large intestine (cecum, colon, and rectum) and anus. Also present are accessory organs contributing to the digestive process such as the salivary glands, pancreas, gallbladder, liver etc.

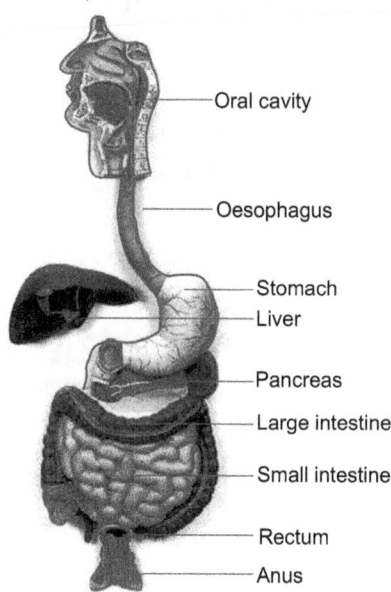

Fig. 4.1 : The General Structure of the Digestive System

Each of these organs plays an important role in the uptake as well as digestion of food. The system comprising of these organs has a variety of enzymes involved in the breakdown and digestion of food stuff. The main function of this system is digestion of food particles and absorption of digestive contents (nutrients, electrolytes, minerals, and fluids) - into the circulatory system for cellular use. Undigested material passes through the lower intestinal tract with the aid of peristalsis to the rectum and anus and is excreted as faeces or stool.

The digestive system comprises of two types of organs –

(a) Digestive organs

(b) Accessary digestive organs

Functions of the Digestive System

1. To ingest food
2. To transport food
3. To digest food into simpler components that can be absorbed and utilised by the body.
4. To absorb necessary nutrients into the blood stream.
5. To expel waste from the body

Any disorder or dysfunction of any of these component organs leads to a variety of symptoms and ailments. It is well said and established that a healthy GIT system contributes greatly to the well-being of a person.

There are a variety of disorders and ailments associated with the GIT, ranging from minor to serious and there are many therapies including, drug therapy to cure them.

Some minor symptomatic ailments are curable by the use of some drugs of inorganic compositions. Most of these drugs are available over the counter (OTC), without prescription. Therefore, they need to be dealt with care by the pharmacist in particular. The pharmacist should be able to make judgment between a minor ailment and a serious ailment and accordingly decide on the usage of these drugs.

These drugs of inorganic origins are mainly divided in 5 main categories (thus, in scope of this chapter), namely;

Inorganic agents used to treat gastrointestinal disorders include-

1. **Products for altering gastric pH :** Acidifying Agents: Used to treat achlorhydria (absence of HCl in the gastric secretion) e.g.- Dilute HCl.

2. **Antacids:** Used to treat hyperchlorhydria and peptic ulcer.

3. Protectives for intestinal inflammation.

4. Adsorbents for intestinal toxins.

5. Cathartics or laxatives for constipation.

4.2 Acidifying Agents

The process of gastric acid secretion occurs at the level of the parietal cells of oxyntic glands in the gastric mucosa of stomach through the stimulation of any of the three receptors; muscarinic -M_1 receptors, gastrin receptors, histamine-H_2 receptors, producing 2-3 litres of gastric juice per day (HCl of *pH* 1).

Acid secretion is a physiologically important process of the stomach as;

1. Gastric acid induces activation pepsinogen,converting it into pepsin (protolytic enzyme). This enzyme is formed at the acidic pH and is responsible to initiate digestive process

2. Gastric acid kills bacteria and other microbes ensuring a stable intragastric environment.

3. Gastric acid softens the fibrous food and converts it into forms suitable for digestion.

Thus, if there is lack of sufficient gastric acid in the stomach it can cause GIT disturbances.

Achlorhydria or anacidity is the condition, which occurs due to the absence of HCl in the gastric secretion.

There are two types of achlorhydrias :-

1. Gastric secretion is devoid of HCl even after the stimulation with histamine phosphate. This condition occurs in gastritis or gastrectomy.

2. In the second case there is lack of HCl, but it may be secreted upon the administration of histamine phosphate. This second condition occurs in chronic nephritis, alcoholism etc.

Symptoms of achlorhydria range from mild diarrhea, epigastric pain, sensitivity to spicy/pungent food, to even pernicious anemia due to lack of intrinsic factor, leading to poor absorption of B_{12}.

4.2.1 Dilute Hydrochloric Acid I.P. (HCl : M. Wt. 36.46)

It is given in the treatment of achlorhydria. It contains 10% w/w HCl. This dilute HCl is prepared by mixing 274g of HCl and 726g of purified water. It occurs as clear colourless, and odourless liquid strongly acidic to litmus.

The acid should be diluted with 50 volumes of water or juice and sipped through a glass tube to prevent its direct action on the dental enamel.

Assay: An accurate amount of HCl is transferred to a conical flask containing 40ml of water and the solution is titrated with 1N NaOH using methyl orange as an indicator.

Each one ml of 1N NaOH is equivalent to 0.036g of HCl.

Use : Dilute HCl is used as gastric acidifier when the level of HCl in the gastric juice is low. Since, it is not clear that the decrease of gastric HCl content is due to any specific cause or is a symptom associated with many physiological conditions, it is doubtful whether the administration of dilute hydrochloric acid will serve any useful clinical purpose.

4.3 Antacids

The walls of the stomach are lined with cells that secrete mucus, pepsinogen and hydrochloric acid. The hydrochloric acid concentration of the stomach ranges from 0.03 M to 0.003 M which corresponds to a pH range of about 1.5 to 2.5. The mucus lining of the stomach protects the stomach walls from the action of stomach acid. When excess acid is produced, a condition known as acid indigestion results. If excess acid is forced into the esophagus acid reflux or "heart burn" results. High acid concentrations can damage the stomach lining resulting in ulcers. Excess stomach acid results in a state of discomfort known as acid indigestion or heartburn. If the condition remains neglected it may lead to peptic ulcers of various types. Today hyperacidity is linked mainly to "Hurry, Worry & Curry", though, there can also be other pathological reasons.

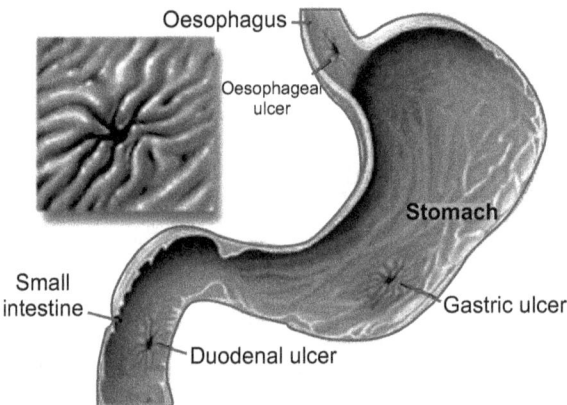

Fig. 4.2 : Different types of ulcers due to hyperacidity

Acid indigestion may results from a variety of factors including -

- Overeating
- Alcohol consumption
- Eating certain foods
- Anxiety
- Smoking
- Certain Drugs, like NSAID's i.e., Aspirin, Ibuprofen, Diclofenac etc.

Compounds employed in therapy to treat these conditions are known as **Antacids**.

Antacid drugs give relief to pain due to hyper acidity. The beneficial effects of antacids are due to two mechanisms i.e., neutralisation of gastric juice and reduction in protolytical activity of pepsin. Elevation of the pH of the gastric content to more than pH 4-5 results in inactivation of enzyme pepsin and at this pH, the damaging effect of the gastric acid to the mucosa is minimum.

Characteristics of an ideal antacid –

1. It should not be absorbed in systemic circulation
2. It should not cause systemic alkalosis.
3. It should neither be a constipative nor laxative.
4. It should produce rapid and long lasting effect.
5. Its reaction with gastric acid should not cause evolution of large quantities of CO_2 gas.
6. It should be palatable and inexpensive.
7. It should inhibit pepsin

Classification of Antacids: These are broadly classified into three categories;

- Inorganic Antacids
- H_2 - Receptor Antagonists
- Proton Pump Inhibitors (PPI)

Alternatively, antacids are classified as follows -

(1) On pharmacological basis –

    (a) Systemic or absorbable : These are soluble, readily absorbable and capable of producing systemic electrolyte disturbances. E.g. , $NaHCO_3$.

    (b) Non systemic or non-absorbable : They are not absorbed and act exclusively in the GIT. E.g., Calcium containing, (e.g., $CaCO_3$), Aluminium containing (e.g., $Al(OH)_3$), Magnesium containing (e.g., $MgCO_3$).

(2) On the basis of inorganic elements :

    (a) Aluminium containing antacids : E.g., Aluminium hydroxide gel, Aluminium phosphate gel etc.

    (b) Calcium containing antacids : $CaCO_3$, tribasic Calcium phosphate.

    (c) Mg containing antacids : Mg tri silicate, $MgCO_3$, milk of magnesia ($Mg(OH)_2$) ,MgO etc.

    (d) Na containing antacids : $NaHCO_3$.

    (e) Combined antacids –

        (i) Aluminium hydroxide and $Mg(OH)_2$ gel.

        (ii) Aluminium hydroxide gel and Mg tri silicate.

The inorganic compounds are used as antacids since a long time in the therapy and they still enjoy the faith of physicians and patients for symptomatic relief. These are weak bases that are used to neutralise excess stomach acid.

Reactions of Inorganic Antacids

Antacids react with HCl in the stomach

Some common antacid reactions include -

$$CaCO_3 + 2HCl \rightarrow CaCl_2 + H_2O + CO_2$$
$$NaHCO_3 + HCl \rightarrow NaCl + H_2O + CO_2$$
$$Al(OH)_3 + 3HCl \rightarrow AlCl_3 + 3H_2O$$
$$Mg(OH)_2 + 2HCl \rightarrow MgCl_2 + 2H_2O$$
$$MgO + 2HCl \rightarrow MgCl_2 + H_2O$$

Some of the common antacids are -

(a) Aluminum Hydroxide Gel (IP) : Molecular formula : Al(OH)$_3$, M. Wt: 78.

It is a hydrated suspension of aluminum oxide with variable amounts of basic aluminum carbonate. It contains not less than 3.5 % and not more than 4.4% w/w Al_2O_3.

Preparation

It is prepared by addition of a hot solution of potash alum to hot solution of sodium carbonate.

$$3Na_2CO_3 + KAl(SO_4)_2 + 3H_2O \rightarrow 3Na_2SO_4 + K_2SO_4 + 3CO_2 + 2Al(OH)_3$$
$$\text{potash alum}$$

Properties

Aluminum hydroxide gel is a white viscous suspension. It reacts with gastric acid to give $AlCl_3$ which causes nausea and vomiting.

$$3HCl + Al(OH)_3 \rightarrow AlCl_3 + 3H_2O$$

It's a very popular antacid and causes neutralisation of gastric acid (H_3O^+), by the following mechanism;

$$Al(OH)_3 + 3H_2O \rightarrow [Al(OH)_3.(H_2O)_3]$$
$$[Al(OH)_3.(H_2O)_3] + H_3O^+ \rightarrow [Al(OH)_2.(H_2O)_4]^+ + H_2O$$
$$[Al(OH)_2.(H_2O)_4]^+ + H_3O^+ \rightarrow [Al(OH).(H_2O)_5]^{++} + H_2O$$
$$[Al(OH).(H_2O)_5]^{++} + H_3O^+ \rightarrow [Al(H_2O)_6]^{+++} + H_2O$$

Applications

1. Used as a slow acting antacid to treat hyperacidity.

2. Effective for use in treatments of ulcers and hyperchlorhydria.

Dose

Around 7.5 ml - 15 ml, 4-6 times a day. This 7.5 ml to 15 ml amounts to approximately 150-300 mg of aluminium hydroxide.

Tests for Purity

The following tests are carried out to test for purity :

1. pH (Its pH should be between 5.5 and 8.),
2. Arsenic,
3. Heavy metals,
4. Chloride,
5. Sulphate,
6. Neutralising capacity or acid consuming capacity,
7. Microbial limits.

Assay

An accurately weighed quantity of the gel is dissolved in concentrated hydrochloric acid by warming and diluted with water. To an aliquot of 10ml, a known excess of 0.05M disodium edetate is added and the mixture is neutralised with 1M sodium hydroxide using methyl red as indicator. This neutral mixture is warmed on a water bath for half an hour to ensure complexation of aluminium by sodium edetate. Hexamine is added and it is back titrated with 0.05M lead nitrate using xylenol orange as indicator.

Each ml of 0.05M disodium edetate $\cong 0.002549g$ of Al_2O_3.

Notes: *This is a complexometric titration and the sodium edetate is allowed to complex aluminium under conditions where metals such as calcium and magnesium do not interfere. The excess of sodium edetate left after complexation with aluminium is over, is back titrated with 0.05M lead nitrate solution. Hexamine is added to raise the pH to the alkaline side to facilitate the complexometric titration of the excess of EDTA with 0.05M lead nitrate.*

(b) Aluminum Phosphate : Molecular formula: $AlPO_4$, M. Wt.: 122

Official as Dried Aluminum Phosphate Gel (N.F. & B.P.)

It consists mainly of about 80% of hydrated aluminum orthophosphate.

Preparation

By interaction between aqueous aluminum chloride and sodium phosphate.

$$AlCl_3 + Na_3PO_4 \rightarrow AlPO_4 + 3NaCl$$

Properties

It is a white powder or suspension having friable aggregates and contains not less than 80% aluminum phosphate ($AlPO_4$). Practically insoluble in ethanol, water, alkali hydroxide solutions, but soluble in dilute mineral acids. The gel has pH 6.0-7.2.

The acid neutralising capacity is based on the release of trivalent phosphate ion due to its strongly basic nature.

$$AlPO_4 \leftrightarrow Al^{+3} + PO_4^{-3}$$

Applications

Used as a mild slow acting antacid having half the acid neutralising capacity of aluminum hydroxide gel.

Dose

5-15 ml (1 teaspoonful to 1 tablespoonful).

Assay

Weighed quantity of sample is dissolved in 100 ml HCl and to 10 ml of an aliquot of this is added 25ml 0.05 M disodium edetate, made alkaline by ammonia solution and boiled for 10 minutes to ensure complexation. Ammonium acetate (1.55 g) and glacial acetic acid (6 ml) are added and volume made to 100 ml with water and pH adjusted to 4.5. Finally dithizone 2ml (0,025% w/v) is added and the solution titrated against 0.05M $ZnCl_2$ until red end point. A blank is performed alongside to get the difference in amount of disodium edetate consumed by the sample.

Each ml of 0.05M disodium edetate$\cong$ 0.006098 g $AlPO_4$

Tests for Purity

1. Acidity and alkalinity,
2. Arsenic,
3. Heavy metals,
4. Phosphate

Storage

Store in a well closed container.

(c) Basic Aluminium Carbonate : Molecular formula: $Al(OH)CO_3$, M. Wt. : 104.03

It occurs as a gel and works similar to aluminium hydroxide gel. The dietary phosphate is excreted as aluminium phosphate in the faeces and made unavailable to form the phosphatic calculi.

Preparation

Preparation of basic aluminium carbonate involves reaction between stoichiometric amounts of aluminum hydroxide gel and sodium bicarbonate in aqueous solution

$$Al(OH)_3 + Na_2CO_3 \rightarrow Al(OH)CO_3 + 2NaOH$$

Assay

By complexometric titration, similar to aluminum hydroxide gel under similar conditions adopting same procedure and reagents.

Each ml of 0.05M disodium edetate $\cong$ 0.0039 g of $Al(OH)CO_3$

Application

It is suggested for the management of phosphatic urinary calculi.

(d) Calcium Carbonate : Synonym Precipitated Chalk : Molecular formula: $CaCO_3$, M.Wt.: 100.09

It contains not less than 98% and not more than 100.5% $CaCO_3$ calculated on dried basis.

Preparation

1. Prepared by mixing solutions of calcium chloride and sodium carbonate

$$CaCl_2 + Na_2CO_3 \rightarrow CaCO_3 + 2NaCl$$

2. It can also be prepared by passing carbon dioxide through lime water

$$CaO + CO_2 \rightarrow CaCO_3$$

Properties

It is a white, odourless, tasteless microcrystalline powder. It decomposes back to CaO and CO_2 when heated beyond 83°C. Its water solubility is enhanced in the presence of CO_2.

$$CaCO_3 + H_2O + CO_2 \rightarrow Ca(HCO_3)_2$$

Assay

Calcium carbonate is assayed by complexometric titration under alkaline medium. Sample is dissolved in aqueous HCl and the volume of the resultant clear solution is adjusted to 250 ml. To a 50 ml aliquot is added 100 ml water and the pH is adjusted to 12-15 with 1 N NaOH. The solution is titrated against 0.05M EDTA using murexide-naphthol green indicator to a deep blue end point.

Each ml of 0.05M EDTA ≅ 0.0051 g of $CaCO_3$

Applications

1. Used as a fast acting non-systemic antacid.
2. As a supplement for calcium deficiency.
3. As dentifrices due to mild abrasive property and in cosmetics.

(e) Magnesium Carbonate (Heavy & Light) : $[(MgCO_3).Mg(OH)_2.5H_2O]$ and $[(MgCO_3).Mg(OH)_2.3H_2O]$

It is hydrated basic magnesium carbonate containing 40-45% magnesium oxide.

Preparation

Magnesium carbonate is prepared by mixing hot solutions of magnesium sulphate and sodium carbonate

$$5MgSO_4.7H_2O + 5Na_2CO_3.10H_2O \rightarrow (MgCO_3)_4.Mg(OH)_2.5H_2O + 5Na_2SO_4 + 5O_2 + 7H_2O$$

Or simply as

$$MgSO_4 + Na_2CO_3 \rightarrow MgCO_3 + Na_2SO_4$$

Properties

Both light and heavy magnesium carbonates are hydrated. Both are white, odourless powders practically insoluble in water and alcohol. When heated to redness both give MgO.

$$3[(MgCO_3).Mg(OH)_2.5H_2O] \rightarrow 4MgO + 3CO_2 + 6H_2O$$

Applications

1. Used as a mild non-systemic antacid.
2. Used as a mild laxative

Identification Tests

1. Reactions with glacial acetic acid,
2. Assay for purity,
3. Residue on ignition (NLT 42% and NMT 45% w/w on dried basis),
4. Test for soluble matter (insoluble residue NMT 10 mg / gm sample).

Assay

Magnesium carbonate is assayed by complexometric titration under alkaline medium. Sample (1 g) is dissolved in HCl and resultant clear solution is adjusted to a volume of 250 ml with water. To 50 ml of this solution is added 100 ml water and 15 ml aqueous NaOH to adjust the pH to alkaline. The solution is titrated against 0.05M EDTA using murexide-naphthol green indicator to a deep blue end point.

Each ml of 0.05M EDTA $\cong 0.002015$ g of $MgCO_3$

(f) Magnesium Oxide (Heavy and Light) : Molecular formula : MgO, M. Wt. 48.3

It contains not more than 98% of MgO.

Preparation

1. Prepared by heating magnesium carbonate to redness

$$MgCO_3 \rightarrow MgO + CO_2$$

2. Similarly, it is also prepared from both light and heavy types of magnesium carbonates by heating them red hot.

$$3[(MgCO_3).Mg(OH)_2.3H_2O] \rightarrow 4MgO + 3CO_2 + 4H_2O$$

$$3[(MgCO_3).Mg(OH)_2.5H_2O] \rightarrow 4MgO + 3CO_2 + 6H_2O$$

Properties

Both light and heavy magnesium oxides are white, odourless powders practically insoluble in water and alcohol. In presence of acid the oxides get converted to hydroxides.

$$MgO + 2 H_3O^+ \rightarrow Mg(OH)_2 + 2H_2O$$

It neutralises gastric acid.

$$MgO + 2HCl \rightarrow MgCl_2 + H_2O$$

Applications

1. Used as a mild non-systemic antacid.
2. Used as a cathartic.

(g) Magnesium Hydroxide : (Milk of Magnesia) - Molecular formula: $Mg(OH)_2$, M. Wt. : 68

It contains 95.0 to 100.5% of $Mg(OH)_2$.

Preparation

1. It is either obtained from light magnesium oxide and water in presence of NaOH.

$$MgO + H_2O \rightarrow Mg(OH)_2$$

or

2. Through the action of magnesium sulphate and sodium hydroxide.

$$MgSO_4 + 2NaOH \rightarrow Mg(OH)_2 + Na_2SO_4$$

Properties

It is a bulky white odourless powder insoluble in water or alcohol, but soluble in dilute acids. Milk of Magnesia is a gelatinous translucent suspension with creamy white consistency. Water may separate out on standing.

Applications

1. Used as an antacid.
2. It is also used as a laxative. It is preferred over magnesium oxide.

Tests for Purity

1. Characteristic tests for Mg,
2. **Test for purity :** Magnesium hydroxide is tested for (i) soluble alkalis, (ii) soluble carbonates, (iii) acid insoluble matter, (iv) Tests for As, Ca, and heavy metals. (v) Alkalinity, (vi) Soluble salts, (vii) Microbial count.

Assay

Weighed amount of sample is dissolved in 25 ml of 1N H_2SO_4. Excess of acid is back titrated against 1N NaOH using methyl red indicator.

Each ml of 1N $H_2SO_4 \cong 0.02917$ g of $Mg(OH)_2$

(h) Magnesium Trisilicate : (Hydrated magnesium silicate) – Molecular formula : $2MgO.3SiO_2.3H_2O$; M. Wt.: 260.86

It contains magnesium oxide and silicon oxide with varying proportions of water of crystallisation. It has not less than 29% and not more than 32% of MgO and not less than 65% and not more than 68.5% of SiO_2

Preparation

It is prepared from sodium silicate and magnesium sulphate. When the solution of the later is run slowly in the former, magnesium trisilicate is precipitated, which is filtered, washed, dried and powdered.

$$2MgSO_4 + 4NaSiO_2 + excess\ 3H_2O \rightarrow 2MgO.3SiO_2.3H_2O + 2Na_2SO_4 + SiO_2$$

Properties

Magnesium trisilicate is a odourless, tasteless, white grainy and slightly hygroscopic powder. Practically insoluble in water and alcohol.

$$MgO + 2 H_3O^+ \rightarrow Mg(OH)_2 + 2H_2O$$

It neutralises gastric acid.

$$MgO + 2HCl \rightarrow MgCl_2 + H_2O$$

Applications

1. Used as an antacid and adsorbent. It reduces gastric pain and hyperacidity.
2. Used in larger doses to induce diarrhoea.
3. Due to the presence of silicon dioxide, it acts as a protectant for gastric mucosa in ulcers.

Tests for Purity

1. Test for heavy metals,
2. Tests for chloride, sulphate,
3. Loss on ignition,
4. Test for acid absorption capacity,
5. Test for free alkali,
6. Test for soluble salts.

Dose

1 gm four times a day.

Assay

(i) **For Magnesium Oxide:** Complexometric titration. By dissolving accurately weighed sample in dilHCl, diluting with water, adjusting pH with NaOH to alkaline, and titrating it against 0.05M disodium edetate using murexide indicator – napthol green to deep blue end point.

Each ml of 0.05M disodium EDTA $\cong$ 0.002015 g of MgO

(ii) **For silicon dioxide:** Gravimetric titration. Accurately weighed sample is treated with 1N H_2SO_4 by heating for prolonged time and filtered. The supernatant is filtered and residue washed with water, digested, dried and incinerated on a platinum crucible. Thereafter, HF and H_2SO_4 are added. Then, it is evaporated and ignited to dryness to give the weight of SiO_2.

(i) Sodium Bicarbonate : (Baking Soda) – Molecular formula : NaHCO₃, M. Wt.: 84.01

Sodium bicarbonate contains NLT 99.0% and NMT 100.5% of $NaHCO_3$, calculated on dry basis.

Preparation

Laboratory scale: By continuously passing CO_2 gas through aqueous NaOH solution and concentrating it to dryness.

$$2NaOH + CO_2 \;\rightarrow\; Na_2CO_3 + H_2O + CO_2 \rightarrow 2NaHCO_3$$

Industrial scale: By Solvay process involving interaction between ammonia, carbon dioxide and brine solution as follows. The later saturated with ammonia is passed through carbonating column at temperature below 15°C. The precipitated $NaHCO_3$ is filtered out and dried.

$$NH_3 + NaCl + H_2O + CO_2 \rightarrow NH_4HCO_3 + NaCl + H_2O \rightarrow NH_4Cl + NaHCO_3 + H_2O$$

However, purity is not as good as that produced by using NaOH.

Properties

It is a white crystalline or opaque powder, highly soluble in water, but practically insoluble in alcohol. It is odourless with saline taste. Its solution is alkaline and when treated with acids it gives effervescence due to release of CO_2.

Applications

1. Used as an antacid with rapid onset and short duration of action. Its reaction with HCl leads to release of CO_2 which results in flatulence.

2. It is also used as a systemic alkaliser.

3. It is used as an electrolyte replinisher.

4. It is an important constituent of effervescent mixtures

5. It finds many applications in food products. E.g. Baking soda, Eno fruit salt etc.

Tests for Purity

1. Identification (reactions of Na and CO_3),

2. pH (1% w/v solution has pH NMT 8.6),

3. Clarity and color of solution,

4. Loss on drying (NMT 0.25%),

5. Ammonium compounds (No evolution of NH3 when warmed with NaOH solution).

Dose

300 mg to 2 gm four times a day.

Assay

1 g sample dissolved in 20 ml water and resultant solution is titrated against 0.5N H_2SO_4 using methyl orange as an indicator.

Each ml of 0.5N$H_2SO_4 \cong 0.042$ g of $NaHCO_3$

4.3.1 Combination Antacids

1. None of the antacids has all the properties of an ideal antacid.

2. Calcium and Aluminium antacids cause constipation.

3. Magnesium antacids reduce constipation but have laxative action.

4. Most of the market preparations contain combinations of antacids in order to approach an ideal.

5. These combinations balance both the constipative (Al and Ca) and laxative (Mg) side effects of antacids.

6. In some mixtures of two antacids, one has rapid onset of action, while other has prolonged action.

Some examples of Combination Antacids:

1. Aluminum hydroxide gel + magnesium hydroxide (Cremalin^R) - A suspension containing both agents in 2-4% w/v.

2. A very popular combination of aluminum and magnesium hydroxides, known as Magaldrate (hydrated magnesium aluminate).

3. Aluminum hydroxide gel + magnesium trisilicate combination (GelusilR). This is often combined with simethicone, a defoaming agent to get relief from flatulence.

4. Aluminum hydroxide gel + calcium carbonate. This shows both rapid and prolonged action.

5. Multiple Antacid Combinations. E.g. Algicon Tablets/Suspension have 4 antacids combination. It contains,

    (a) Aluminum hydroxide gel   -   360 mg

    (b) Magnesium alginate   -   500 mg

    (c) Magnesium carbonate   -   320 mg

    (d) Potassium bicarbonate   -   100mg

4.4 Protectives and Adsorbents

These are chemically inert agents commonly used for treatment of mild diarrhea or dysentery or other GIT disturbances due to their ability to absorb gases, chemical and drug poisons and bacterial toxins. These agents mainly include bismuth compounds, kaolin, activated charcoal and pectin.

Bismuth compounds: These are traditionally used for their mild astringent, antacid, antiseptic actions and protective effects on the mucous membranes. These include bismuth subcarbonate, bismuth subnitrate, bismuth subsalicylate, bismuth subgallate, etc.

(a) Bismuth subcarbonate : Molecular formula : $[(BiO_2)_2(CO_3)]_2.H_2O$

It is a basic carbonate of bismuth which on ignition yields NLT 90% and NMT 92% of BiO_3 calculated on a dry basis.

Preparation

By reaction of bismuth nitrate and sodium carbonate in aqueous medium

$$4Bi(NO_3)_3 + 6Na_2CO_3 + H_2O \rightarrow [(BiO_2)_2(CO_3)]_2.H_2O + 2NaNO_3 + 4CO_2\uparrow$$

Properties

White or pale yellow, odourless and tasteless powder, insoluble in water and alcohol but dissolves in HCl. Decomposes into yellow Bi_2O_3, when ignited.

Tests for Purity

1. Identification (reactions of Bi and CO_3),
2. Tests for purity: Loss on drying (NMT 2% w/w),
3. Tests for chloride, sulphate and nitrate,
4. Tests for heavy metals, Pb, As, Ag, Cu etc.

Dose

1 to 3 gm in divided doses.

Assay

By gravimetric method. Accurately weighed sample is ignited in a tared crucible to constant weight. The bismuth trioxide (Bi_2O_3) so obtained is cooled and weighed.

Applications

1. As astringent and absorbent in the treatment of diarrhea, dysentery, ulcerative colitis
2. As a mild antacid
3. As a topical protective

(b) Kaolin : It is hydrated aluminum silicate occurring as soft white or off white powder or lumps. It has clay like taste and odour particularly when moistened. It is insoluble in water, alcohols, acids and alkali. It occurs in two forms, heavy and light.

Applications

1. It is normally used as an absorbent in combination of pectin.
2. It is used to reduce GIT and mucal inflammations.
3. It is used in topically applied dusting powders

(c) Pectin : It is produced commercially as a white to light brown powder, mainly extracted from citrus fruits, and is used in food as a gelling agent, particularly in jams and jellies. It is also used in fillings, medicines, sweets, as a stabiliser in fruit juices and milk drinks, and as a source of dietary fiber. It is mainly used for treating diarrhoea in combination with kaolin as an adsorbent and protectant combination. It works by absorbing excess fluids and reducing intestinal movement.

(d) Activated charcoal: It is a residue from the destructive distillation of various organic materials treated specially to increase its absorptive power. It is a fine black, odourless tasteless powder free from gritty matter. It is used as an absorbent in the treatment of diarrhoea. It is also used as an antidote in drug poisoning.

4.5 Saline Cathartics

Cathartics are agents which quicken, increase and facilitate the evacuation (defecation) from the bowel. The milder forms are called as **Purgatives** and still milder forms are available which are for frequent use and they are **Laxatives.**

They are the most widely used OTC medications (Over The Counter; which do not require medical prescription).

All three are generally administered by oral route and some times by rectal route (enema or suppository). They all act by retaining the body fluid and do not cause excessive dehydration.

Cathartics act by 4 mechanisms;

1. Through local irritation of G.I.T. directly and thereby stimulating peristaltis. These are called as **stimulants.** E.g., Rhubarb, senna, podophyllum, castor oil, bisacodyl etc.
2. Through increasing the bulk of intestinal contents and thereby stimulating peristaltis. E.g., **Bulk purgatives** like ispagol, CMC, gums etc.
3. By acting as **lubricants** of the GIT and thereby facilitating smooth evacuation of feces. E.g., Liquid paraffin, glycerine, mineral oils etc.
4. By increasing osmotic load of intestine by absorbing water and thereby stimulating peristaltis. These are **saline cathartics.** E.g., sodium phosphate, magnesium sulphate, sodium potassium tartarate, magnesium carbonate etc.

(a) Sodium phosphate : (Disodium phosphate, dibasic sodium phosphate, disodium hydrogen phosphate) – Molecular formula : $Na_2HPO_4 \cdot 7H_2O$ ($12H_2O$), M.Wt.: 268.07 (358.14).

Contains NLT 98.5 % and NMT 101.0% Na_2HPO_4 on dried basis.

Preparation

It is prepared by the action of phosphoric acid on sodium carbonate. Neutralisation and concentration of the solution yields colourless granular salt.

$$H_2PO_4 + Na_2CO_3 \rightarrow Na_2HPO_4 + H_2O + CO_2$$

Properties

It is colourless white granular salt. It effervesces in dry air. It is freely soluble in water and slightly soluble in alcohol. Its aqueous solution is basic in nature.

Purity

1. **Identification Tests :** 10 % w/v solution should give confirmatory tests for sodium and phosphate.
2. **pH :** 2% aqueous solution should be 9-12,
3. **Tests for purity :** Heavy metals as well as Ca, Mg and ions like chloride, sulphate and loss on drying.

Assay

Sample solution in water is tritrated against 0.5N H_2SO_4 using bromocresol green indicator to a green colour end point.

$$2Na_2HPO_4 + H_2SO_4 \rightarrow 2NaH_2PO_4 + Na_2SO_4$$

Each ml of 0. 5N H_2SO_4 ≅ 0.0071 g of Na_2HPO_4

Applications

1. Because of its poor absorption in the GIT it is considered safe and is the widely used saline cathartic (laxative).

2. It is an important component of phosphate buffer

(b) Sodium potassium tartrate : (Rochelle salt) - Molecular formula: $C_4H_4O_6NaK.4H_2O$ M. Wt. : 282.2

CHOHCOONa

| · 4H$_2$O

CHOHCOOK

It has NLT 99.0% and NMT 104.0% of $C_4H_4O_6NaK.4H_2O$

Preparation

Sodium potassium tartrate is prepared by the action of potassium bitartrate on sodium carbonate in boiling water. Neutralisation by evolution of CO_2 followed by concentration of the solution yields colourless white salt.

$$2KHC_4H_4O_6 + Na_2CO_3 + 6H_2O \rightarrow 2C_4H_4O_6NaK.4H_2O + CO_2$$

Properties

Sodium potassium tartarate appears as colourless white crystals often coated with white powder. It effervesces in dry air. It has a cooling saline taste. It is freely soluble in water and practically insoluble in alcohol. Its aqueous solution is basic in nature.

Purity

1. **Identification tests :** 10 % w/v solution should give confirmatory tests for sodium and potassium; On heating emits odour of burn sugar and residue is alkaline to litmus giving effervescence with acids.

2. **Tests for purity :** Heavy metals such as As, Fe as well as chloride, sulphate and loss on drying,

3. **Acidity and alkalinity** by titrating against standard NaOH and HCl solutions using phenolphthalein as indicator.

Assay

Gravimetric – Volumetric : Accurately weighed sample is carbonized in a silica crucible, the residue boiled with 15 ml 0.5N H_2SO_4 and filtered. Filtrate is diluted to 50 ml with water and excess acid titrated with 0.5 N NaOH using methyl orange indicator.

Each ml of 0. 5N$H_2SO_4 \cong 0.071$ g of $C_4H_4O_6NaK.4H_2O$.

Applications

1. Because of its poor absorption in the GIT, it is considered safe and is the widely used saline cathartic (laxative).

2. It is an important component of effervescent powders and is an important food additive.

(c) Magnesium carbonate: (Magnesite) –Molecular formula: $MgCO_3$, M.Wt. 84.31

Properties

It is an inorganic salt that is a white solid. Several hydrated and basic forms of magnesium carbonate also exist as minerals. Magnesite consists of white trigonal crystals. The anhydrous salt is practically insoluble in water, acetone, and ammonia. All forms of magnesium carbonate react with acids to release CO_2.

Preparation

Magnesium carbonate is ordinarily obtained by mining the mineral magnesite. Magnesium carbonate can be prepared in the laboratory by reaction between any soluble magnesium salt and sodium bicarbonate

$$MgCl_2 + 2NaHCO_3 + H_2O \rightarrow MgCO_3(s) + 2NaCl + H_2O + CO_2$$

High purity industrial routes include a path through magnesium bicarbonate - combining magnesium hydroxide and carbon dioxide. A slurry of magnesium hydroxide is treated with 3.5 to 5 atm. of carbon dioxide below 50 °C, giving the soluble bicarbonate, then vacuum drying the filtrate, which returns half of the carbon dioxide as well as water.

$$Mg(OH)_2 + 2CO_2 \rightarrow Mg(HCO_3)_2$$
$$Mg(HCO_3)_2 \rightarrow MgCO_3 + CO_2 + H_2O$$

Applications

1. A laxative to loosen the bowels, and colour retention in foods.
2. High purity magnesium carbonate is used as antacid,
3. As an additive in table salt to keep it free flowing.
4. It is an important food additive known as E504.

(d) Magnesium sulphate : (Epsom Salt) : $MgSO_4.7H_2O$ M. Wt. 246.5

It is having NLT 99% and NMT 100% of $MgSO_4$ calculated on dried basis.

Preparation

The heptahydrate can be prepared by neutralising sulphuric acid with magnesium carbonate or oxide, but it is usually obtained directly from natural sources. Anhydrous magnesium sulphate is prepared only by the dehydration of a hydrate.

$$MgCO_3 + H_2SO_4 \rightarrow MgSO_4 + CO_2 + H_2O$$

Properties

It is colourless white powder highly soluble in water, but insoluble in alcohol. It has cool saline taste. The anhydrous form is strongly hygroscopic, and can be used as a desiccant.

Purity

1. **Identification Tests :** 10 % w/v solution should give confirmatory tests for magnesium and sulphate;

2. **Tests for purity :** Heavy metals As, Fe as well as chloride, sulphate and loss on drying.

3. **Acidity and alkalinity :** 1 g sample dissolved in 10 ml water should yield a clear solution neutral to litmus.

Assay

An aqueous solution of accurately weighed sample made alkaline with ammonia-ammonium chloride buffer is titrated against 0.05 M disodium edetate to blue end point using Mordant Black 11 indicator.

Each ml of 0. 05M disodiumedetate $\cong 0.00602$ g of $MgSO_4$.

Applications

1. Magnesium sulphate is a common pharmaceutical preparation of magnesium, commonly known as Epsom salt, used both externally and internally. Epsom salt is used in bath salts and for isolation tanks.
2. Oral magnesium sulphate is commonly used as a saline laxative or osmotic purgative.
3. Magnesium sulphate is the main preparation of intravenous magnesium and also used an anticonvulscant.

Question Bank

1. Justify the role of acidifying agents in medical treatment as well as physiology.
2. Enumerate the role of gastric acid in the body
3. Classify and briefly discuss the important categories of gastro-intestinal agents.
4. What are antacids ? Classify them and discuss the characteristics of an ideal antacid.
5. What are combination antacids and discuss some important combinations.
6. What is the role of simethicone in antacid preparations.
7. Name the inorganic compound or combination involved in the following; (Fill in the blanks).

Synonym or Brand Name	Inorganic compound or combination involved
1. Baking Soda	
2. Rochelle salt	
3. Epsom salt	
4. Gelusil	
5. Gelusil MPS	
6. Magnesite	
7. Magaldrate	
8. Milk of Magnesia	

8. Write a note on any one class of inorganic antacids
   (i) Aluminium, (ii) Magnesium, (iii) Sodium.

9. Discuss saline cathartics with respect to their definition, role , mechanism of action and classification in detail with suitable examples

10. Give a brief monograph of any one of the following important inorganic GIT agents
    - (i)   Aluminum hydroxide gel
    - (ii)   Magnesium Oxide
    - (iii)   Calcium Carbonate
    - (iv)   Magnesium Carbonate
    - (v)   Magnesium Hydroxide,
    - (vi)   Magnesium Trisilicate,
    - (vii) Sodium Bicarbonate.

11. Discuss in detail the GIT agents catagorised as protectives and adsorbents

12. Write short notes on -
    - (i)   Bismuth compounds,
    - (ii)   Bismuth subcarbonate,
    - (iii)   Kaolin,
    - (iv)   Activated charcoal,
    - (v)   Pectin.

13. Discuss any one of the following saline cathartics in details:
    - (i)   Sodium phosphate,
    - (ii)   Sodium potassium tartarate,
    - (iii)   Magnesium carbonate,
    - (iv)   Magnesium sulphate

✍ ✍ ✍

Chapter **5**...

Electrolytes: Extra and Intracellular Ions

Contents ...

5.1 Introduction

5.2 Chloride (Cl⁻)

5.3 Phosphate (PO_4^{2-})

5.4 Bicarbonate (HCO_3^-)

5.5 Sodium (Na⁺)

5.6 Potassium (K⁺)

5.7 Calcium (Ca⁺⁺)

5.8 Magnesium (Mg⁺⁺)

5.9 Electrolytes used for Replacement Therapy

    5.9.1 Sodium Replacement

    5.9.2 Potassium Replacement

    5.9.3 Calcium Replacement

    5.9.4 Magnesium Replacement

5.10 Calculation of mEq/l, m osmol/l of electrolyte

5.11 Physiological Acid-Base Balance

5.12 Electrolytes used in Acid-Base Therapy

5.13 Electrolyte Combination Therapy

• Question Bank

5.1 Introduction

Inorganic and organic solutes are present in body fluids to maintain the optimum activity of cells and tissues. The electrolytes are ionic constituents of body fluid. Body maintains its normal physiological state and the process is called **"Homeostatis".** It is essential for the control of pH, osmotic balance and ionic balance. The normal homeostatis is disturbed in many disease conditions leading to ionic or osmotic imbalance.

There are a large number of products under the general heading, Replacement Therapy, which can be prescribed by physicians as and when required to correct electrolyte imbalance. Electrolytes used for replacement and acid base correction therapy are cations with very specific biochemical functions found only in trace amounts. The sodium and chloride are found in the plasma and intestinal fluids while, potassium, magnesium and phosphate are found in the intracellular fluid.

Major Physiological Ions

There are seven physiological ions which are called as electroytes and which play a crucial role in the normal functioning of the human body. These are not only essential for maintaining homeostatis but, they also perform varied functions, which include regulation of acid-base balance, regulation of osmotic pressure, biochemical reactions and important physiological functions :

(i) Chloride, (ii) Phosphate, (iii) Bicarbonate, (iv) Sodium, (v) Potassium, (vi) Calcium and (vii) Magnesium.

The electrolytes are categorised as intracellular ions and extracellular ions as follows −

Intracellular Ions	Extracellular Ions
(i) Potassium	(i) Sodium
(ii) Magnesium	(ii) Chloride
	(iii) Calcium
	(iv) Phosphate
	(v) Bicarbonate

5.2 Chloride (Cl⁻)

It is a major extracellular anion and is responsible for maintaining proper hydration, osmotic pressure and anion-cation balance in vascular and intestinal fluid compartments. The main source of chloride anion is food and it is absorbed completely from the intestinal tract. It is excreted by the kidney through glomerular filtration and reabsorbed by tubules.

The deficiency or excess of chloride in the body causes **hypochloremia** and **hyperchloremia**, respectively.

Hypochloremia : It may be caused by;

(a) Inflammation of kidney (nephritis).

(b) Metabolic acidosis in diabetes mellitus.

(c) Renal failure.

(d) Prolonged vomiting.

Hyperchloremia : This condition is seen in dehydration, decreased renal blood flow in congestive heart failure and excessive chloride intake.

5.3 Phosphate (PO_4^{-2})

Phosphate (PO_4^{-2}) is the principal anion of the intracellular fluid compartment. Nearly, 80% of the total body phosphate is found in bones whereas, 15% in soft tissues. Phosphorous in the form of phosphate is essential for normal bone and tooth development. It is also essential for proper calcium metabolism. Phosphorous can exist in both organic and inorganic forms. Organic forms include phospholipids and various organic esters.

The dihydrogen phosphate ($H_2PO_4^-$) anion is absorbed from the intestines. This form is found in the stomach and upper part of the duodenum.

Most of the phosphate salts of pharmaceutical concern are derived from phosphoric acid (H_3PO_4). This acid is also known as *ortho*-phosphoric acid and represented as follows :

$$
\begin{array}{c}
O \\
\uparrow \\
HO - P - OH \\
| \\
OH
\end{array}
$$

ortho-phosphoric acid

The prefix '*ortho*' indicates the highly 'hydroxylated' known form of acid.

Metaphosphoric acid is obtained from orthophosphoric acid, when, it loses one water molecule. It is represented as

$$H_3PO_4 \xrightarrow{\ OH^-\ } HPO_3 + H_2O$$

$$
\begin{array}{c}
O \\
\uparrow \\
O \leftarrow P - OH
\end{array}
$$

meta-phosphoric acid

Sodium metaphosphate (Graham's salt), a polymer is commonly employed as a water softening agent. Pyrophosphoric acid is obtained by the dehydration of two molecules of *ortho*-phosphoric acid.

$$
\begin{array}{c}
O \qquad\quad O \\
\uparrow \qquad\quad \uparrow \\
HO - P - O - P - OH \\
| \qquad\quad\; | \\
OH \qquad OH
\end{array}
$$

Pyrophosphoric acid

The formulae for other phosphate salts are as follows –

(a) **NaH_2PO_4** : Sodium dihydrogen phosphate or sodium biphosphate.

(b) **Na_2HPO_4** : Sodium monohydrogen phosphate or sodium biphosphate.

(c) **Na_2PO_4** : Sodium phosphate.

Serum phosphate levels usually correlate with serum calcium values. Whenever calcium concentrations are not within normal range, serum phosphate will either be too high or too low. The increase in serum phosphate levels can cause **hyperphosphatemia** and low serum phosphate levels lead to **hypophosphatemia**.

Hyperphosphatemia : It may be found in the following conditions

(a) Increase intestinal phosphate absorption along with calcium leads to hypervitaminosis D.

(b) Renal failure.

(c) Hypoparathyroidism (lack of paran-thyroid hormone).

Hyperphosphatemia may cause kidney stone due to phosphatic urinary calculi.

Hypophosphatemia : It may be seen in following conditions :

(a) **Rickettsia (Vitamin D deficiency) :** Decreased intestinal absorption of phosphate and calcium.

(b) **Hyperthyroidism :** Inhibition of renal tubular phosphate reabsorption due to increased levels of parathyroid hormone.

(c) Long term antacid therapy.

5.4 Bicarbonate (HCO$_3^-$)

Bicarbonate is the most important anion in the acid-base balance buffer system. It is the second most prevalent anion of the extracellular fluid compartment. The lack of bicarbonate results in metabolic acidosis and excess causes metabolic alkalosis. The sodium salt of bicarbonate, sodium bicarbonate ($NaHCO_3$) is used to neutralise excess of acid present in the stomach, when taken orally.

5.5 Sodium (Na$^+$)

It is the principal cation responsible for maintaining normal hydration and osmotic pressure. More than adequate amount of sodium is present in our daily diet with complete absorption from the intestinal tract. Excess of sodium is excreted by the kidneys, which makes them the ultimate regulators of the sodium content of the body. The homeostatic mechanisms for controlling plasma osmolality is largely determined by serum sodium concentration. The sodium and water balance are closely related and disorders of sodium and water are potentially serious.

The disorders of sodium may cause

(a) Hyponatremia

(b) Hypernatremia

(c) Hypertension

(d) Edema

(a) Hyponatremia : (Low serum sodium levels) The known reasons for hyponatremia are :

1. Diabetes insipidus (disease of the pituitary gland).

2. Metabolic acidosis where sodium is excreted.

3. Addison's disease - decreased excretion of anti-diuretic hormone and aldosterone.

4. Kidney damage.

5. Diarrhoea and vomiting.

(b) Hypernatremia : (Increased serum sodium level). It is found in :

1. Cushing's syndrome - increased aldostrone production.

2. Severe dehydration.

3. Certain types of brain injuries.

4. Excess treatment with sodium salts.

(c) Hypertension : There is a proven correlation between sodium content of the tissue and hypertension. Less sodium intake in diet is advised in hypertensive patients.

(d) Edema : If body is unable to eliminate sodium, the concentration starts to increase, water is retained and edema results. The patient can take on a puffy appearance and swelling. The build up of fluid puts an added burden on the heart.

5.6 Potassium (K^+)

It is the major intracellular cation and its concentration is 23 times higher in the extracellular fluid compartments. Total body potassium content is approx. 50 mEq/kg body weight. The sodium potassium ATPase is the major cellular enzyme responsible for maintaining very low intracellular Na concentration and increased intracellular potassium concentration.

Potassium is rapidly absorbed from diet. Any excess of potassium is excreted by kidneys. Both elevated and low serum potassium levels cause hyperkalemia and hypokalemia, respectively.

Hyperkalemia : It is less common and usually occurs during certain types of kidney damage. In same conditions, potassium is retained in the body and can also lead to acid-base imbalance.

Hypokalemia : Low serum potassium levels can cause changes in ECG and myocardial function. It results in flaccid and weak muscles and low blood pressure. It can occur due to overuse of thiazide diuretics and alkalosis.

5.7 Calcium (Ca^{++})

It is the most important electrolyte of the extracellular fluid compartments and 99% of body calcium is found in the bones and teeth. Calcium is absorbed from the upper part of the small intestine. The actual absorption of calcium across the intestinal membrane is controlled by the parathyroid hormone and a metabolite of vitamin D. It is believed that, cholecalciferol (Vitamin D_3) is hydroxylated at C-25 position in the liver and C-1 position in the kidneys. This activated metabolite 1, 2, 5-dihydrocholecalciferol, may function as a gene activator. Causing the synthesis of a calcium-binding protein, which transfers the calcium cation across the intestinal wall.

Milk is the main source of dietary calcium. Lactose present in milk plays a role in calcium absorption. Calcium absorption and distribution takes place under parathyroid hormone and calcitonin.

Functionally, 99% of all body calcium is supportive and found in bones as hydroxyapatite. The remaining ionic calcium is involved in neurohormonal functions, blood clotting, muscle contraction and other biochemical process. Calcium is necessary for the release of acetylchloride from preganglionic nerve endings.

The diseases related to calcium metabolism and deficiency are

(a) Hypercalcemia

(b) Hypocalcemia

(c) Osteoporosis

(d) Paget's disease

(e) Rickettsia

(a) Hypercalcemia : It is found in hyperparathyroidism, hypervitaminosis D, and some bone neoplastic diseases. Symptoms are fatigue, muscle weakness, constipation, anorexia (loss of apetite) and cardiac irregularities.

(b) Hypocalcemia : It can be caused by hypoparathyroidism, Vitamin D deficiency, bone cancer, Cushing's syndrome (hyperactive adrenal cortex), acute pancreatitis and acute hyperphosphatemia.

(c) Osteoporosis : It is a serious condition of bone degeneration commonly associated with ageing. The bone become weaker and more fragile.

The probable causes of osteoporosis are –

1. Problems associated with intestinal calcium absorption.

2. Vitamin D deficiency.

3. Menopausal estrogen loss in women.

4. Ageing.

(d) Paget's disease : This disease is due to faulty calcium metabolism, characterised by an initial phase of decalcification and softening of bone and deformity.

(e) Rickettsia : This disorder is characterised by abnormalities in calcitrol synthesis.

5.8 Magnesium (Mg^{++})

It is the most important and the fourth most abundant cation in the body. 50% of total body magnesium is combined with calcium and phosphorus in bone. It is an essential component of many of the enzymes involving phosphate metabolism.

Magnesium is also indispensible for protein synthesis and for the smooth functioning of the neuromuscular system. Most of the magnesium absorption takes place in the acid medium of the duodenum. Symptoms of magnesium deficiency include personality changes, failure to weight gain and cardiac disturbances. Hypomagnesia and alkalosis have been correlated with the withdrawal symptoms of chronic alcoholics. Hypermagnesia may lead to hypotension, sedation, muscle paralysis, respiratory depression and complete heart block.

5.9 Electrolytes used for Replacement Therapy

The following salts are used in different formulations such as tablets, injections, elixir, etc.

1. Sodium chloride
2. Potassium chloride
3. Potassium gluconate
4. Calcium chloride
5. Calcium gluconate
6. Calcium lactate
7. Dibasic calcium phosphate
8. Tribasic calcium phosphate
9. Magnesium sulphate.

5.9.1 Sodium Replacement

The intention of sodium replacement is to raise serum sodium concentration to 120 mEq/l in hyponatremias. There are a variety of sodium chloride preparations such as isotonic solutions used for wet dressings and injections. In all sodium replacement preparations, the main constituent is sodium chloride. Additionally, the solutions may contain dextrose, potassium chloride, mannitol fructose, lactates, calcium salts, etc.

The following sodium chloride preparations are used for sodium replacements.

(i) **Sodium chloride injection :** It is 0.9% NaCl solution sterlised and used topically to clean the wounds and body cavities, as an intravenous infusion, sterile vehicle, as well as, isotonic vehicle.

(ii) **Sodium chloride tablets :** Available as 600 mg, 1 gm and 2.25 gm tablets as electrolyte replenisher.

(iii) **Dextrose and sodium chloride injection :** It is a sterile solution of sodium chloride (0.2 – 0.9% w/v) and dextrose (2.5 - 20% w/v) used as fluid, nutrient and electrolyte replenisher.

(iv) **Dextrose and sodium chloride tablets :** Usually available as tablets of 200 mg of sodium chloride (3.42 mEq) and 450 mg dextrose for use as electrolyte and nutrient replenisher.

(v) **Mannitol and sodium chloride injection :** It is a sterile infusion of (5 - 20% w/v) of mannitol sodium chloride (0.3 - 0.45% w/v) used as diuretic when given by IV route.

(vi) **Fructose and sodium chloride injection :** It is a sterile infusion of 10% fructose and 0.5% sodium chloride given by IV and subcutaneous routes of administration as a fluid, nutrient and electrolyte replenisher.

(vii) **Ringer's injection :** It is an IV infusion containing 0.86%. NaCl (147 mEq/l Na, 4 mEq/lk, 4.5 mEq/l Ca, 155.5 mEq/l Ca) used as an electrolyte replenisher.

(viii) Lactated Ringer's injection : It contains 0.6% NaCl (130 mEq/lNa, 4 mEq/l k, 2.7 mEq/l Ca, 109.7 mEq/l Cal, 27 mEq/l lactase) used as systemic alkalizer. It is contra-indicated in alkalosis conditions.

5.9.2 Potassium Replacement

Potassium chloride (KCl) is the drug of choice for oral replacement as a diluted solution. It is irritating to gastro-intestinal tract, so tablet dosage form is not recommended. To make the taste of oral solution of potassium chloride, it is mixed with fruit or vegetable juices.

Potassium chloride is indicated in hypopotassemia, Menier's syndrome (disease of inner ear which includes dizziness and noise in the ear) and antidote in digitalis intoxication.

Potassium therapy is contraindicated in patients with impaired renal function, acute dehydration and in patients receiving potassium-sparing diuretics.

The usual dose of KCl is 1 gm four times a day.

The following potassium chloride preparations are used for potassium replacement.

1. **Potassium chloride injection :** It is a sterile solution available as 1.5 gm in 10 ml; 3 gm in 20 ml and 4.5 and 6 gm in 30 ml of water for injection.
2. **Potassium chloride tablets :** Available as 300 mg or 1 gm enteric coated tablets.
3. **Ringer's injection :** It is an intravenous infusion that contains 0.3 % KCl (147 mEq/l Na, 4 mEq/lk, 4.5 mEq/l Ca, 155.5 mEq/l Cl) and is used as electrolyte replenisher.
4. **Lactated ringer's injection :** It is 0.3% KCl with 27 mEq/l of lactate used as systemic alkalizer and electrolyte replenisher.
5. **Potassium gluconate elixir :** It is an elixir of 4.68 gm of potassium gluconate is 15 ml, equivalent to 20 mEq of potassium.
6. **Potassium gluconate tablets :** These are sugar coated tablets of 1.17 gm of potassium gluconate equivalent to 5 mEq of potassium.

5.9.3 Calcium Replacement

Calcium chloride ($CaCl_2$) is the main source of calcium in many commercially available electrolyte replacements, whereas, calcium gluconate is considered in the treatment of choice for hypocalcemia because it is non-irritating when given orally and intravenously.

Calcium carbonate and calcium silicate are used orally as antacids.

The following commercially available preparations of calcium available for calcium replacements are.

1. **Ringer's injection :** It contains 0.033% $CaCl_2.2H_2O$ (147 mEq/l Na, 4 mEq/l k, 4.5 mEq/l Ca, 155.5 mEq/l Cl) in the infusion form as electrolyte replenisher.
2. **Lactated Ringer's injection :** It is an IV infusion used as systematic alkalizer and electrolyte replenisher.
3. **Calcium gluconate injection :** It is 97 mg/ml of calcium gluconate available as 10 ml ampoule
4. **Calcium gluconate tablets :** These are available as 500 mg and 1 gm tablets.

5. **Calcium lactate tablet :** These are tablets of 300 mg and 600 mg of calcium lactate pentahydrate. Its dose is 1 - 5 gm three times a day.

6. **Dibasic calcium phosphate :** It is an oral source of calcium and phosphorous used in pregnancy and in lactation available in the powder form. The usual dose is 1 gm three times a day.

7. **Tribasic calcium phosphate :** It is an antacid used in the dose of 1 - 5 gm three times a day.

5.9.4 Magnesium Replacement

Magnesium sulphate is the major source of magnesium replacement available as magnesium sulphate injection. It is available as 1 gm in 2 ml; 2 gm in 20 ml and 15 gm in 30 ml as IV infusion fluid. It is used for the prevention of recurrent seizures in pregnant women. It is also used in myocardial infarction and premature labour. Dried magnesium sulphate paste is used as an application to inflammatory skin conditions such as boils and carbonucles.

5.10 Calculation of mEq/*l*, m osmol/*l* of electrolyte

To understand the calculations of milliequivalent and milliosmolality, the student shall understand some basic terminologies :

(a) Molality

(b) Molarity

(c) Millimole

(d) Equivalent weight

(e) Milliequivalent

(f) Osmolality

(g) Osmolarity

(a) **Molality :** 1 molal solution as gram-equivalent weight of a substance when dissolved in 1000 gm of solvent.

(b) **Molarity :** Molarity is defined as gram-equivalent weight of a substance when dissolved in 1000 ml of solvent.

(c) **Millimole :** Millimole is defined as a gram molecular weight of a substance in milligrams when dissolved in 1000 ml of solvent.

(d) **Milliequivalent :** Milliequivalent is defined as one thousandth (10^{-3}) of a gram equivalent of a chemical element, ion or electrolyte.

(e) **Equivalent weight :** It is the weight of the substance which either contributes or reacts with one mole of hydrogen ion in that solution.

$$mEq/l = \frac{mg\ of\ substance/L}{Equivalent\ weight}$$

$$= \frac{mg\ of\ substance/L}{Molecular\ weight}$$

Example : Calculate the number of mEq of sodium chloride in one litre of 0.55% w/v solution.

$$0.55\% \text{ NaCl} = 5.5 \text{ gm of NaCl/L}$$
$$= 5500 \text{ mg of NaCl/L}$$
$$\text{Molecular weight of NaCl} = 23 + 35.5 = 58.5$$
$$\text{mEq}/l = \frac{5500}{58.5} = 94.01 \text{ mEq NaCl/L}$$

As number of sodium ions is equal to chloride ions, the concentration of each ion is equal i.e. 94.01 mEq Na^+/l and 94.01 mEq Cl^-/l.

5.11 Physiological Acid-Base Balance

The body fluids have balanced quantity of acids and bases. The maintenance of this balance is necessary for biochemical reactions that occur the body, because biochemical reactions are very sensitive to even small changes of acids and bases.

Example : Low pH value in stomach is required for functioning of enzyme pepsin which is necessary for the digestion of food.

The pH values of certain body fluids are as follows -

1. **Blood :** 7.4 - 7.5
2. **Semen :** 7.2 - 7.6
3. **Bile :** 6.0 - 8.5
4. **Saliva :** 5.4 - 7.5
5. **Urine :** 4.5 - 8.0
6. **Gastric juice :** 1.5 - 3.5

Body has its own buffer system which prevents drastic change in the pH value of blood. It also helps to convert strong acids and bases into weak acids or bases. Lungs and kidneys are the main body organs which help to maintain systems in the body.

In case of low respiration, the accumulated carbon dioxide carbines with water and forms carbonic acid which releases hydrogen ions and causes acidosis.

$$CO_2 + H_2O \longrightarrow H_2CO_3 \longrightarrow H^+ + HCO_3^-$$

In over breathing, excessive excretion of CO_2 occurs and causes alkalosis.

Kidney has the ability to generate ammonia which neutralises acidic byproducts of protein metabolism and excrete in urine.

There are two major buffer systems in the body -

(i)   Bicarbonate (HCO_3^-) : Carbonic acid system

(ii) Monohydrogen phosphate (HPO_4^{-2}) : Dihydrogen system ($H_2PO_4^-$)

The bicarbonate buffer systems found in the plasma and kidney whereas, phosphate buffer system is found in the cells and kidneys.

The following steps are involved in acid excretion by kidneys -

(a) Sodium salts of mineral and organic acids are removed form the plasma by glomerular filtration.

(b) Sodium is preferentially removed form the renal filtrate or tubular fluid, called as $Na^+ - H^+$ exchange.

$$Na^+ + H_2CO_3 \longrightarrow Na^+ + HCO_3^- + H^+$$

(c) The sodium bicarbonate returns to the plasma and protons enter the tubular fluid forming acids of the anions that originally were sodium salts.

Potassium excretion is very complex and will be decreased when the sodium reaching the distal tubule is low or the proton secretions by kidney tubule is increased.

The formation of ammonia from protein and amino acid metabolism is another means of removing protons.

5.12 Electrolytes used in Acid-Base Therapy

Electrobytes are used in acid-base therapy to treat metabolic acidosis and alkalosis. Sodium salts of bicarbonate, lactate, acetate and citrates are used to treat metabolic acidosis, where as ammonium salts are used to treat metabolic alkalosis.

The following salts are used in acid-base imbalance -

1. Potassium citrate
2. Potassium acetate
3. Sodium bicarbonate
4. Sodium acetate
5. Sodium citrate
6. Ammonium chloride.

(I) Sodium Acetate

Molecular formula : $CH_3COONa.3H_2O$,   **Molecular weight :** 136.08

Physical Properties

It is colourless, odourless, white granular crystalline powder, very soluble in water and soluble in alcohol.

Preparation

It is prepared by neutralising acetic acid with sodium carbonate or bicarbonate. The solution is filtered and the filtrate obtained is concentrated by evaporation to yield sodium acetate crystals.

$$2CH_3COOH + Na_2CO_3 \longrightarrow 2CH_3COONa + H_2O + CO_2 \uparrow$$
$$CH_3COOH + NaHCO_3 \longrightarrow CH_3COONa + H_2O + CO_2 \uparrow$$

Uses

It is used to treat uremic acidosis. It is component of peritoneal dialysis fluid.

(II) Potassium Acetate

Molecular formula : CH_3COOK,   **Molecular weight :** 98.15

Physical Properties

It is a colourless, white crystalline powder and has slightly alkaline taste. It is very soluble in water and freely soluble in alcohol.

Preparation

The acetic acid is neutralised with potassium carbonate or bicarbonate till effervescence ends. The solution is evaporated and allowed to solidify. It is powdered and stored immediately.

$$2CH_3COOH + K_2CO_3 \longrightarrow 2CH_3COOK + H_2O + CO_2 \uparrow$$

Uses

It is a systemic and urinary alkalizer. It also has diuretic action. It is used for peritoneal dialysis and haemodialysis.

(III) Potassium Citrate

Molecular formula : $C_6H_5K_3O_7.H_2O$,   **Molecular weight :** 324.4

Physical Properties

It is an odourless, colourless granular powder with saline taste. This salt is stored in air tight container due to its deliquescent nature. It is soluble in water and insoluble in alcohol.

Preparation

The solution of citric acid when neutralised with potassium carbonate or bicarbonate yields potassium citrate subjected to evaporation of solution to dryness.

$$3KHCO_3 + C_5H_8O_7 + H_2O \longrightarrow C_6H_5K_3O.H_2O + 3H_2O + 3CO_2 \uparrow$$

Use

It has diuretic and expectorant action. It also has anticoagulant and slight laxative action.

(IV) Sodium Bicarbonate

Molecular formula : $NaHCO_3$,   **Molecular weight :** 84.01

Physical Properties

It is a white crystalline powder with saline taste. It is soluble in water but insoluble in alcohol.

Preparation

It is prepared by Solvay process on industrial scale. The solution of NaCl (Prime solution) is saturated with ammonia to remove impurities, the solution is filtered and passed through the carbonating tower. It is allowed to react with a current of CO_2 and the tower is cooled to enhance precipitation. The precipitate is filtered out and dried.

$$H_2O + CO_2 \longrightarrow H_2CO_3$$
$$NH_3 + H_2CO_3 \longrightarrow NH_4HCO_3$$
$$NaCl + NH_4HCO_3 \longrightarrow NaHCO_3 + NH_4Cl$$

Uses

It is used as an antacid in systemic acidosis. It is also used in daily cooling process. It is an ingredient of Eno fruit salt. Its action is rapid in relieving acidity.

(V) Sodium Citrate

Molecular formula : $C_6H_5Na_3O_7.2H_2O$,   **Molecular weight :** 297.10

Physical Properties

It is white crystalline powder with saliva taste. It is soluble in water but, insoluble in alcohol and ether.

Preparation

It is prepared by neutralising solution of citric acid with sodium carbonate or bicarbonate. When the effervescence ceases, the solution is evaporated to crystallise the product.

$$
\begin{array}{l}
CH_2COOH \\
| \\
HO - C - COOH + 3\ NaHCO_3 \longrightarrow Na_3C_5H_5O_7.2H_2O + 2H_2O + 3CO_2 \uparrow \\
| \\
CH_2COOH \\
\text{Citric acid}
\end{array}
$$

Uses

It is used as systemic alkalizer. It has anti-coagulant and good sequestering properties. It is also used as an expectorant and as a pharmaceutical aid.

(VI) Ammonium Chloride

Molecular formula : NH_4Cl,   **Molecular weight :** 53.49

Physical Properties

It appears as a hygroscopic white crystalline powder with salina taste. It is soluble in water and alcohol.

Use

It is used as an expectorant and in diuretics.

5.13 Electrolyte Combination Therapy

Electrolyte combination therapy is required when the deficit is severe. The electrolyte combination products are divided into two groups

(i)   Fluid maintenance

(ii) Electrolyte replacement

Intra-venous fluids are intended to supply normal requirements of water and electrolytes to patients who cannot take them orally. All maintenance solutions contain 5% dextrose. This minimises the build up of those metabolites associated with starvation. In addition to dextrose, the general electrolyte composition of maintenance solution is 25 - 30 mEq/l of Na, 15 - 20 mEq/l of K, 22 mEq/l of Cl, 20 - 23 mEq/l of HCO_3, 3 mEq/l of Mg and P.

Replacement therapy is needed when there is heavy loss of water and electrolytes, as in prolonged fever, severe vomiting and diarrhoea. There are usually two types of solutions used in replacement therapy -

1. Solution for rapid initial replacement, and

2. Solution for subsequent replacement.

The rapid initial replacement solution resemble the electrolyte concentration found in extracellular fluids.

The electrolyte composition of initial replacement solutions are -

Electrolyte	m Eq/l
Na	130 - 150
K	4 - 12
Cl	98 - 109
HCO_3	28 - 55
Mg	3
Ca	3 - 5

The electrolyte composition of subsequent replacement solutions are -

Electrolyte	m Eq/l
Na	40 - 121
K	16 - 35
Cl	30 - 103
HCO_3	16 - 53
Mg	3 - 6
Ca	0 - 5
P	0 - 13

Official Combination of Electrolyte Infusion

1. **Ringer's Injection :** Composition of 1 litre IV fluid :

$$NaCl ~-~ 8.6~gm$$
$$KCl ~-~ 0.3~gm$$
$$CaCl_2 ~-~ 0.33~gm$$

This is equivalent to

Electrolyte	m Eq/l
Na	147
K	4
Ca	4.5
Cl	155.5

2. **Lactated Ringer's Injection :** Composition of 100 ml IV fluid is given below

$$NaCl \ - \ 600 \ mg$$
$$Sodium \ lactate \ - \ 310 \ mg$$
$$KCl \ - \ 30 \ mg$$
$$CaCl_2 \ - \ 20 \ mg$$

This is equivalent to

Electrolyte	m Eq/l
Na	130
K	4
Ca	2.7
Cl	109.7
Lactate	27

3. **Oral Electrolyte Solution :** There have been sodium chloride and sodium chloride plus dextrose tablets available for years to replace the salt lost through excessive perspiration. These have been used by people working in climatic conditions who could suffer from the hyponatremic water intoxication syndrome (cramps, fever and confusion). In the last few years, oral electrolyte solutions have been introduced for athletes, to replace fluid and electrolytes lost through excessive perspiration as well as to quench thirst.

Question Bank

1. Define the following terms:
   (a) Molarity
   (b) Molality
   (c) Equivalent Weight
   (d) Osmolarity
   (e) Osmolality
   (f) Millequivalent
2. Give the composition of intra and extra cellular electrolytes.
3. What are intra and extra cellular ions? Give their important physiological roles.
4. Comment on electrolyte replacement therapy.
5. Explain the role of intra and extra cellular ions in maintaining physiological balance.
6. What are electrolytes? Enlist major intra and extra cellular electrolytes.
7. Discuss the role of sodium and potassium as an important electrolytes.
8. Discuss various electrolytes used in sodium, potassium and calcium replacement.

9. What is metabolic acidosis and alkalosis?

10. Comment on functions of Na^+ and K^+ ions in the body.

11. How acid base balance of body is maintained?

12. Enlist the electrolytes used in physiological acid base balance.

13. Write a note on oral rehydration salts (ORS).

14. Explain the role of electrolytes in acid base therapy.

15. Explain the term milliequivalent. Calculate the number of MEq of potassium chloride in one liter of a 0.48% w/v solution.

16. Enlist official sodium chloride formulations used in electrolyte replacement therapy.

17. Explain physiological role of chloride and bicarbonate.

18. How electrolyte combinations are used as replacement therapy? Explain.

19. What do you understand by electrolyte replacement therapy?

20. Write a note on the following:

 (a) Physiological acid–base balance

 (b) Electrolyte used as acid-base therapy

 (c) Electrolyte combination therapy

 (d) Electrolyte replacement therapy

 (e) Pharmaceutical application of electrolytes

 (f) Physiological role of Na^+ and K^+ ions as electrolytes

 (g) Electrolytes replenishes

 (h) ORS.

      ✎ ✎ ✎

Chapter 6...

Essential and Trace Elements

Contents ...

6.1   Introduction
6.2   Trace Elements
    6.2.1   Classification of Trace Elements
6.3   Iron (Fe)
    6.3.1   Transferrin: (Iron Transfer Protein)
    6.3.2   Ferritin: (Iron Storage Protein)
    6.3.4   Official Compounds of Iron
6.4   Copper (Cu)
    6.4.1   Wilson's Disease
    6.4.2   Official Compounds of Copper
6.5   Zinc (Zn)
    6.5.1   Official Compounds of Zinc
6.6   Iodine (I)
    6.6.1   Official Compounds of Iodine
•   Question Bank

6.1 Introduction

The human body requires 7 important food substances to sustain and grow. These are depicted below.

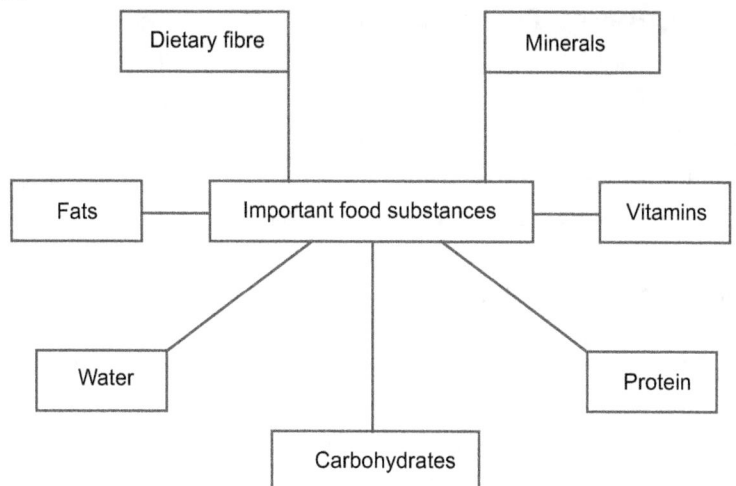

Dietary elements (commonly known as **dietary minerals** or **mineral nutrients**) are the chemical elements required by living organisms, other than the four elements carbon, hydrogen, nitrogen, and oxygen present in common organic molecules. The term "dietary minerals" is archaic, as the substances it refers to are chemical elements rather than actual minerals.

Chemical elements in order of abundance in the human body include the **seven major dietary elements** namely; calcium, phosphorus, potassium, sulphur, sodium, chlorine and magnesium. The other important **"trace"** or **"minor dietary elements"**, necessary for mammalian life, include iron, cobalt, copper, zinc, manganese, molybdenum, iodine, bromine, and selenium.

There are 50 chemical elements identified as important for growth, development and regulation of vital functions. Over twenty dietary elements are necessary for mammals and several more for various other types of life.

These elements or minerals can be further classified as;

- **Major :** Calcium, Phosphorous, Sodium, Potassium, Magnesium
- **Minor :** Required less than a few milligram per day; Iron, Iodine, Fluorine, Zinc, Copper, Cobalt, Chromium, Manganese, Molybdenum, Selenium, Nickel, Tin, Silicon, Vanadium.

6.2 Trace Elements

These are naturally occurring, homogeneous, inorganic substances required by humans in amounts less than 100 mg/day. These can be defined as **essential nutrients** required in trace amounts and are vital for human body.

- To maintain normal yet complex physiological functions related to body's growth and development.
- To balance toxicity levels.

They are also known as micronutrients.

6.2.1 Classification of Trace Elements

Based upon their biological effects, diseases that occur due to their deficiency and toxicity due to overdose, they are categorised as:

1. **Essential :** Iron, Zinc, Copper, Cobalt, Chromium, Fluorine, Iodine, Manganese, Molybdenum and Selenium.
2. **Probably essential :** Nickel, Tin, Vanadium, Silicon, Boron.
3. **Non-essential :** Aluminium, Arsenic, Barium, Bismuth, Bromine, Cadmium, Germanium, Gold, lead, Lithium, Mercury, Rubidium, Silver, Strontium, Titanium and Zirconium.

Essential Trace Elements are further divided into two sub-groups :

1. **Trace Elements :** Iron, Zinc and Copper
2. **Ultra Trace-Elements :** Manganese, Selenium, Cobalt, Chromium, Fluorine, Iodine and Molybdenum.

6.3 Iron (Fe)

Atomic Number : 26; **Atomic Weight :** 55.845

It is a metal in the first transition series. It is by mass the most common element on earth, forming much of earth's outer and inner core.

Significance of Iron

It is one of the most essential trace elements. Adult human body has 4-6 g of iron. Of this 60-70% is present in blood and rest in storage form and is found in the following forms;

- Hemoglobin 68% (Each gm of Hb contains 3.34mg of Iron).
- Ferritin 13%
- Haemosiderin 12%
- Myoglobin 3%
- Iron enzymes ~0.2% (enzymes that require iron as cofactor) : Cytochrome oxidase, Xanthine oxidase and peroxidase, catalase
- Other iron compounds 3.6%

Physiological Functions of Iron

- Iron is a part of all cells and has many different functions
- Heamoglobin that carries oxygen to the cells contains iron.
- Along with folic acid it is essential for brain development.
- Iron is present in myoglobin that facilitates oxygen use and storage in muscles.
- Iron is an integral part of enzyme reactions in various tissues (cyotchromes, catalases, etc.)
- It is required for regulation of body temperature.
- It is required for catecholamine metabolism.
- Iron decreases susceptibility to infections.

Requirements

As body recycles iron from broken RBCs, the daily requirements may be still low.

- 1 mg per day for males (0.6- 0.9 mg may actually suffice)
- 2.5 mg for females (0.7 – 2.0 mg may actually suffice)
- 3.5 mg for females in physiological stress conditions

Dietary Sources of Iron

- **Haem Iron:** Liver, meat, poultry, fish
- **Non-Haem Iron:** Cereals, GLV, Legumes, Nuts, Oil seeds, Dried Fruits, Jaggery

Factors that interfere with absorption are enzymes in the food –

- Phytates, Oxalates, Phosphates, Dietary fibres.
- Ascorbic acid is the most potent enhancer of iron absorption.

Body loss and iron conservation

- Daily excretion:0.9 mg/day (adult);1.3 mg/day (during menstruation in females)
- Iron loss also increases during bleeding and haemorrhage.
- Body conserves iron very well. Only ~1.3 mg/day is absorbed from digested food. However, the absorption increases during growth and pregnancy. In case of iron deficiency the iron absorption from food increases to 4 mg/day.
- Iron is absorbed in Ferrous (Fe^{2+}) form, which is measurable in blood as free iron.

Absorption, Transportation and Disposition of iron

Dietary iron is mainly absorbed in the duodenum, through an active process, involving a protein called **"Transferrin"**. Ferrous ion is absorbed through the intestinal walls and after entering the capillary blood flow, it is oxidised to ferric form, to combine with its transporting protein - transferrin. In the liver and other storage sites it is in bound form to another protein called **"Ferritin"**. When, the threshold concentration is reached (both proteins saturated at all sites and blood), the body iron handling system turns off the intestinal absorption of iron and dietary iron gets egested as such in the faeces.

6.3.1 Transferrin: (Iron Transfer Protein)

Iron binds to transferrin for transportation in plasma after re-absorption, while the storage occurs in hepato-parenchymal cells, reticulo-endothelial cells, bone marrow, liver and spleen. Each transferrin molecule binds to two iron atoms. Transferrin transports iron to various organs and tissues.

Serum iron + amount of iron bound to transferrin = total iron in circulation.

Determination of transferrin can provide total iron binding capacity. Transferrin can be measured by RIA, ELISA and chemiluminescence

6.3.2 Ferritin: (Iron Storage Protein)

It is a protein having 24 subunits of 500kDa, which binds 4000 iron molecules and accounts for a larger iron storage. It synthesised by cells that store iron and is later used to synthesise heme. Ferritin in serum is derived from the breakdown of macrophages of the RES (liver, spleen and bone marrow). Its measurement is used to assess iron stores in the body. Low ferritin levels indicate depletion of iron stores and used as an early indication of iron deficiency. Increased ferritin levels are observed in liver diseases such as hepatitis, liver cirrhosis due to alcohol consumption and hepatic carcinoma. Increased ferritin levels are also observed in leukaemia, Hodgkin's lymphoma and chronic inflammatory disease. Under these conditions, ferritin is released from inflamed tissues or in case of malignancies it's released by tumours. Ferritin can be measured by RIA, ELISA and chemiluminescence.

6.3.3 Iron Deficiency

Occurs in 3 stages

- **First Stage:** Decreased storage without any other detectable abnormalities.
- **Second Stage:** Stores are exhausted, serum ferritin level decreases.
- **Third Stage:** Decrease in haemoglobin percentage.

Implications : This may lead to functional disturbances, decrease in resistance to infections, increase in morbidity and mortality, decreased work performances, impaired cell mediated immunity.

Iron deficiency results in anaemia whose symptoms include -

- Fatigue
- Headache
- Exertional dyspnoea
- Cardiovascular stress
- Poor tolerance to heavy blood loss.

Causes of Iron deficiency

1. Increased loss of blood and iron due to physiological or other conditions.
2. Decreased absorption of iron because of intestinal parasites or some disorders.

Correction of Iron Deficiency

- Oral iron supplements
- 100-200 mg elemental iron daily
- Higher doses are of no benefit
- Ferrous sulphate tablet oral therapy 65mg/tab
- Pregnant women - 100mg/tablet (+ folic acid)

6.3.4 Official Compounds of Iron

(a) Ferrous Sulphate I.P. : (Green Vitriol, Iron Vitriol) : Molecular formula: $FeSO_4, 7H_2O$; Molecular Weight: 278.02.

It should contain NLT 98.0% and NMT 103.35% of $FeSO_4, 7H_2O$.

Preparation

Prepared by dissolving iron dust or filings in excess of dilute H_2SO_4. The iron dissolves with effervescence. When the reaction subsides, the liquid is boiled to concentrate, filtered and cooled thereafter to obtain the crystals, which are filtered and dried at room temperature.

$$Fe + H_2SO_4 + nH_2O \rightarrow FeSO_4, 7H_2O + H_2O + H_2\uparrow$$

Properties

It is a pale, bluish green, crystalline or granular solid, which is odourless with saline metallic astringent taste. It is efflorescent in dry air and may get oxidised to ferric salt $(Fe_4(OH)_2(SO_4)_3)$, having brownish colour. It is acidic to litmus with a pH about 3.7. It is soluble in water, but practically insoluble in alcohol. When heated it decomposes to ferric oxide, sulphur dioxide and sulphuric acid.

$$2(FeSO_4, 7H_2O) \rightarrow Fe_2O_3 + SO_2 + H_2SO_4 + 13H_2O$$

Applications

Used most widely as in the form of oral iron preparations like tablets, capsules, syrups, reconstitutable dry powders, etc. as a hematinic (promoting formation of haemoglobin) to treat iron deficiency, particularly in uncomplicated anaemias.

Dose: 200 mg 2-3 times/day

Tests for Purity

1. Identification (reactions of Fe and SO_4).
2. Acidity (1% w/v solution in water requires NMT 1.0 ml of 0.1 N NaOH, Indicator : Methyl orange),
3. Tested for heavy metals, As, Cu etc.
4. **Test for basic sulphates (Insoluble sulphates) :** May be detected by presence of turbidity in aqueous solution.

Assay

By Redox Titration : Aqueous sample solution is titrated against 0.1 N $KMnO_4$ solution in presence of dil. H_2SO_4 to a coloured end point.

$$2\ FeSO_4 + 2KMnO_4 + 4H_2SO_4 \rightarrow K_2SO_4 + 2MnSO_4 + Fe_2(SO_4)_3 + 4H_2O$$

Each ml of 0. 1N $KMnO_4$ $\cong 0.0291$ g $FeSO_4$, $7H_2O$

(b) Ferric Ammonium Citrate I.P.: Iron Ferric Ammonium Citrate: $C_6H_{5+4y}Fe_xN_yO_7$ Molecular Weight : Variable.

The molecular formula of ammonium iron(III) citrate is variable. It can be prepared by adding $Fe(OH)_3$ to an aqueous solution of citric acid and ammonia.

It exists in two coloured forms. The brown form contains approximately, 9% NH_3, 16.5–18.5% Fe, and 65% hydrated citric acid; the green form contains approximately, 7.5% NH_3, 14.5–16% Fe, and 75% hydrated citric acid. The green type is more readily reduced by light than the brown. The IP specifies a complex, which should contain NLT 20.5% and NMT 22.5 % Fe.

Preparation

Prepared from ferric sulphate, sodium hydroxide, ammonia and citric acid, in a sequential manner.

1. Aqueous solution of ferric sulphate is first reacted with an alkali (NaOH) and not vice versa, thereby resulting in the formation of neutral ferric hydroxide precipitate and not precipitate out the basic ferric hydroxide.

$$Fe_2(SO_4)_3 + 6NaOH \rightarrow 2Fe(OH)_3 + 3Na_2SO_4$$

2. The ferric hydroxide precipitate is collected and washed free of any excess OH⁻ ions. It is then added with stirring to the solution of citric acid, wherein most of it goes into solution.

$$xFe_2(SO_4)_3 + C_6H_8O_7 \rightarrow Fe(C_6H_8O_7)_3xFe(OH)_3$$

3. To this a slight excess of ammonia is added and any undissolved ferric hydroxide is filtered out. The clear reddish filtrate is concentrated by evaporation with stirring. Little ammonia solution is added to replenish its loss. The resultant thick syrup is painted on glass plates and dried at 40°C. The dried scales are scrapped off and packed .

$$Fe(C_6H_8O_7)_3 \times Fe(OH)_3 + NH_3 \rightarrow C_6H_5 + 4_yFexN_yO_7$$

Properties

It is a solid with bright brownish–red scales, odourless, having astringent taste. It is soluble in water, but practically insoluble in alcohol. It is deliquescent in moist air and affected by light.

Application

Used most widely used in the form of oral iron preparations like tablets, capsules, syrups and as a hematinic.

Dose

1-3 g / day

Tests for Purity

1. Identification (reactions of ferric ion)
2. When heated with NaOH evolves ammonia.
3. Tested for heavy metals, Pb, Zn, as well as ions like chloride and sulphate.

Assay

By Redox Titration : Aqueous sample solution is acidified with H_2SO_4 and warmed till colour turns yellow. The solution is thereafter cooled and 0.1N $KMnO_4$ added dropwise till pink colour persists (to oxidise all Fe^{+2} to Fe^{+3}). Thereafter an excess of HCl (15 ml) and KI (2 g) are added. The liberated iodine is titrated against 0.1 N $Na_2S_2O_3$ solution in presence of starch indicator.

$$2\ FeCl_3 + 2HI \rightarrow 2FeCl_2 + 2HCl + I_2$$
$$2Na_2S_2O_3 + I_2 \rightarrow Na_2S_4O_6 + 2NaI$$

Each ml of 0.1N $Na_2S_2O_3 \cong 0.00585$ g Fe^{+3}.

(c) Ferric Chloride: (Iron (III) choride, hexahydrate) : $FeCl_3$, $6H_2O$: Mol. Wt.: 270.3

It is used as a 15% w/v solution. Its pH is maintained acidic (below 7) by addition of small amount of HCl to prevent precipitation of ferric hydroxide. But due to poor bioavailability as well as irritant effect on bowel it is not much popular.

Purity

(1) Clarity of solution : Very slightly turbid.

(2) Free acid : Weigh 2.0 g of ferric chloride, dissolve in 5 ml of water, and bring a glass rod wetted with aqueous ammonia close to it. No white fumes are evolved.

(3) Nitrate : Treat with aqueous ammonia followed by addition of 5 ml of water, 0.1 ml of indigo carmine TS, and 10 ml of sulphuric acid. A blue colour persists for not less than 5 minutes.

(4) Sulphate not more than 0.019% as SO_4.

(5) Heavy metals: Not more than 20 μg/g as Pb.

(6) Zinc: Not more than 30 μg/g as Zn.

(7) Arsenic: Not more than 4.0 μg/g as As_2O_3.

(8) Free chlorine: Weigh 2.0 g of ferric chloride, dissolve in 5 ml of water, heat, and bring a filter paper wetted with zinc iodide–starch TS close to it. No blue colour develops.

Assay

Weigh accurately about 0.6 g of ferric chloride, transfer into a flask with a ground-glass stopper and dissolve in about 50 ml of water. Add 3 ml of hydrochloric acid and 3 g of potassium iodide, immediately stopper tightly, allow to stand for 15 minutes in a dark place, and titrate with 0.1 mol/l sodium thiosulphate (indicator: starch TS). Perform a blank test in the same manner, and make any necessary corrections.

Each ml 0.1 mol/l $Na_2S_2O_3 \cong 27.030$ mg of $FeCl_3 \cdot 6H_2O$.

Applications

1. Hematinic
2. Laboratory reagent.

(d) Iron sorbitex injection (B.P.)

It contains NLT 4.75 % and NMT 5.25 % w/v Ferric iron .

It is a sterile colloidal solution of complex of ferric iron with sorbitol and citric acid. Sorbitol along with dextran are used to stabilise it.

It is a dark brown clear liquid with a pH between 7.2 - 7.9.

It is administered by intramuscular route to patients who don't respond to oral iron therapy as well as anaemia in advanced pregnancy.

Assay

It is assayed by redox titration. Ferric is reduced to ferrous by zinc amalgam, under acidic pH (H_2SO_4) and then titrated against ceric ammonium sulphate using ferroin sulphate indicator.

Each ml of 0.1N ceric ammonium sulphate $\cong 0.00585$ g Fe^{+3}.

6.4 Copper (Cu)

Atomic Number: 29; **Atomic Weight:** 63.546.

Copper is a ductile transition d-block element (metal) of with very high thermal and electrical conductivity. Pure copper is soft and malleable; a freshly exposed surface has a reddish-orange colour. It is used as a conductor of heat and electricity, a building material, and a constituent of various metal alloys.

Copper is essential to all living organisms as a trace dietary mineral because it is a key constituent of the respiratory enzyme complex cytochrome c-oxidase. The main areas where copper is found in humans are liver, muscle and bone. Copper compounds are used as bacteriostatic substances, fungicides, and wood preservatives.

Source, transportation and storage

- Copper is the third most abundant trace element in the human body.
- The daily dietary requirement is between 2-6mg which is mainly obtained from red meat, cocoa, shell-fish, water pumped through copper pipes and chocolates.
- Typically 40-60% copper is absorbed by the duodenum and is transported via metalloenzymes e.g., ascorbic acid oxidase.
- In plasma, 90% is bound to a conjugated metalloenzyme known as ceruloplasmin, 9% is bound to carrier proteins such as albumin and only 1% is free Cu^{2+}.
- Body content of copper is 80-120mg.

Physiological functions of copper

- Copper is involved in the process of erythropoiesis, erythrocyte function and regulation of erythrocyte survival.
- Copper is critical for energy production in the cells. It is also involved in nerve conduction, connective tissue, the cardiovascular system and the immune system.
- Copper is closely related to oestrogen metabolism and is required for female fertility and to maintain pregnancy.
- Copper stimulates production of the neurotransmitters such as epinephrine, norepinephrine and dopamine.
- Acts as a catalyst for copper-containing enzymes such as; ceruloplasmin, ascorbic acid, dopamine-β-hydroxylase, superoxide dismutase (Cu/Zn-SOD), cytochrome c oxidase (COX),monoamino oxidase, lysyloxidase and tyrosinase.

Absorption and Uptake

- The absorption in gastrointestinal tract requires a specific mechanism of metal binding protein **metallothionein** (Cu^{2+} ions are highly insoluble).
- **Ceruloplasmin** (CP) is a glycoprotein, copper-dependent ferroxidase (95% of the total copper in human plasma), oxidises Fe^{2+} to Fe^{3+} in gastrointestinal iron absorption mechanism.

Metbolism : Model of Cu uptake and metabolism in hepatocytes

Cu crosses the plasma membrane through Ctrl1 (copper transporter1) or DMT1 (divalent metal transporter1) to the trans Golgi network (TGN) by chaperone Hah1. Chaperone protein Ccs delivers Cu to cytosolic Cu/Zn SOD. Cox17 delivers Cu to mitochondria for cytochrome *c* oxidase.

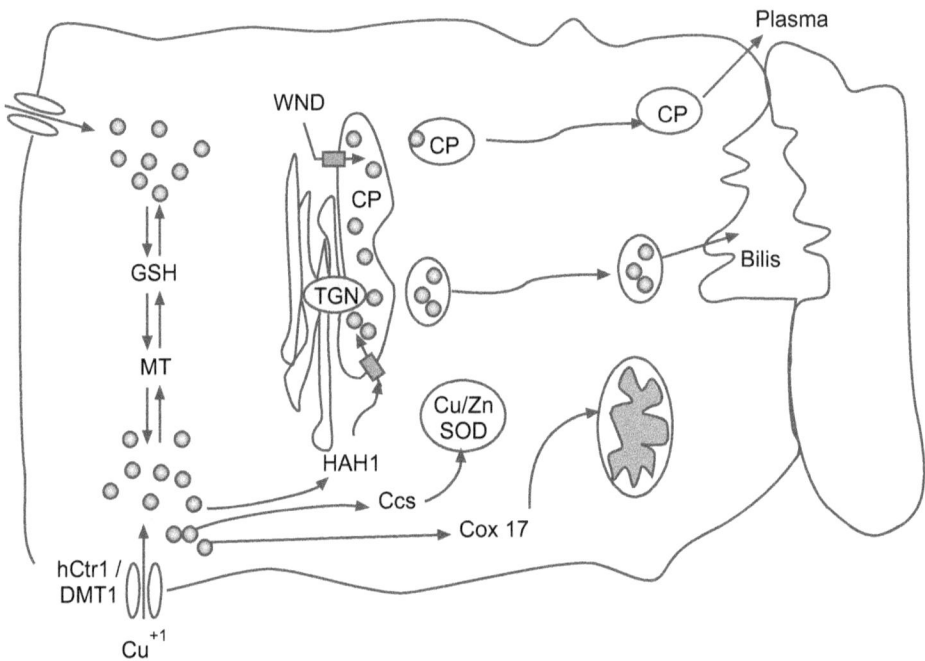

Clinical Significance

Hypocuperaemia is associated with -

- Anemia in infants
- Malnutrition in infants
- Menkes'kinky-hair syndrome: A genetic disorder where copper absorption leads to a brain disease which then cause characteristic wiry-steel hair.
- Nephrosis
- Hypoproteinemia.

Hypercuperaemia is associated with -

- Pregnancy
- Oestrogen therapy
- Thalassemia and anaemia
- Leukaemia and Lymphoma particularly Hodgkin's disease
- Rheumatoid arthritis

Copper toxicity may occur due to ingestion of excess copper or as a result of environmental exposure and this is characterised by increased tissue and serum levels.

6.4.1 Wilson's Disease

It is an autosomal recessive genetic disorder with the onset in the 2nd or 3rd decade.

Serum ceruloplasmin and serum copper is low.

There is increased urine and tissue copper due to excessive deposition of copper in tissues particularly in the hepatocytes and basal ganglia of the brain leading to their steady degeneration.

Symptoms

In the CNS: Tremors, poor coordination, ataxia, rigidity, dysphagia.

In the liver: Jaundice, weakness, partial hypertension, cirrhosis, anorexia.

Normal Values of Cu: Serum = 12-26 µmol/L; Urine = 0.05-0.55 µmol/day.

6.4.2 Official Compounds of Copper

(a) Copper Sulphate : (Cupric Sulphate, Blue Vitriol, Bluestone) : $CuSO_4 \cdot 5H_2O$: Molecular Weight: 249.685

It contains not less than 98.5% and not more than 104.5% of $CuSO_4 \cdot 5H_2O$

Properties

Deep blue triclinic crystals, or blue, crystalline granules or powder which effloresces slowly in dry air. It exists as a series of compounds that differ in their degree of hydration. The anhydrous form is a pale green or gray-white powder, whereas, the pentahydrate ($CuSO_4 \cdot 5H_2O$), the most commonly encountered salt, is bright blue.

Preparation

Copper sulphate is produced industrially by treating copper metal with hot concentrated sulphuric acid or its oxides with dilute sulphuric acid.

$$2Cu + 2H_2SO_4 + O_2 \rightarrow 2CuSO_4 + 2H_2O$$

Identification

1. Solu ility: Freely soluble in water; slightly soluble in ethanol.

2. Passes tests for copper and sulphate.

3. **Acidity :** Dissolve 1 g of the sample in 20 ml of water. A clear blue solution should be obtained. Add 0.1 ml of methyl orange TS solution. The solution should turn brownish green.

4. **pH:** A solution of the sample is acidic to litmus.

5. Insoluble matter should not be more than 50 mg/kg.

6. **Nitrogen compounds:** Not more than 10 mg/kg,

7. **Alkali and rare earths:** Not more than 0.2%,

8. **Lead:** Not more than 10 mg/kg,

9. Other b metals: Not more than 50 mg/kg (as Ni).

Assay (Iodometry)

Weigh 1 g of the sample to the nearest 0.1 mg, and dissolve in 50 ml of water. Add 4 ml of acetic acid and 3 g of potassium iodide and titrate the liberated iodine with 0.1 N sodium thiosulphate, using starch TS as the indicator. Perform a blank determination and make any necessary correction.

Each ml of 0.1 N sodium thiosulphate is equivalent to 24.97 mg of CuSO$_4$ · 5H$_2$O.

Applications :

Copper sulphate is used as

1. An antidote for phosphorous poisoning.
2. A fungicide, algicide and astringent.
3. A laboratory reagent in Fehling's solution and Benedict's reagent.

6.5 Zinc (Zn)

Atomic Number: 30; **Atomic Weight:** 65.38.

Zinc is the first element of group 12 of the periodic table. In some respects, zinc is chemically similar to magnesium: its ion is of similar size and its only common oxidation state is +2. Zinc is the second most abundant trace element.

It acts in the body mainly as a cofactor for 100 diverse zinc-dependant enzymes such as DNA polymerase, alkaline phosphatase, carboxypeptidase etc. These enzymes mainly regulate normal growth, immune system, cell growth, collagen synthesis, wound healing, bone metabolism, reproduction, taste, smell and vision.

Some important examplesof zinc metalloenzymes are listed below -

• Carbonic anhydrase

• Lactate dehydrogenase

• Glutamate dehydrogenase

• Alkaline phosphatase

• Thimidine kinase

• Matrix metalloproteinases

• Gustin – a protein in saliva plays a major role in taste.

Body content is 2.5 g and is distributed as 60% in muscle, 30% in bone and remaining 10% in other body tissues and organs.

Daily requirement is 3-14 mg, age and sex dependant (infants and children require as little as 3-5 mg whereas, adult males require more than adult females however during lactation demand in females increases to 14mg/day)

Diet rich in zinc includes: red meat, fish and sea food.

Absorption and Excretion

Around 20-30% of the dietary zinc is absorbed mainly by the small intestine. Post absorption it is found in the blood bound to erythrocytes (75-80%), the rest is complexed with albumin, transferrin and immunoglobulins. Zinc is mainly excreted through GIT in the stool and to a lesser extent in urine.

Deficiency

Zinc levels will decrease substantially in patients suffering from leukaemia, liver cirrhosis, hepatitis, sickle cell anaemia, infections, pernicious anaemia and malnutrition.

Deficiency of Zn has serious consequences such as-

- Failure to metabolise of nucleic acids (cell division, growth and differentiation)
- Multisystem dysfunction such as growth retardation, hypogonadism, ophtalmologic, gastrointestinal, neuropsychiatric symptoms.

Common symptoms of zinc deficiency that must be noted include :

In children: Growth retardation and skeletal abnormalities are typical symptoms in which zinc deficiency should be considered.

In adults: Reduced sense of taste and smell, loss of appetite, development of abnormal skin lesions and excessive hair loss.

Normal values for zinc levels are:

Serum: 11-23 mol/L

Plasma: 15.5-19 mol/L

Urine: 12 mol/L

Erythrocytes: 185-200 mol/L

6.5.1 Official Compounds of Zinc

(a) Zinc Sulphate : Molecular formula: $ZnSO_4 \cdot 7H_2O$: Molecular Weight 287.56

Content: Zinc sulphate, when calculated on the anhydrous basis, contains not less than 98.0% of zinc sulphate (ZnSO4 = 161.45).

Preparation

Zinc sulphate is prepared by :

(i) Reacting zinc carbonate with sulphuric acid

$$ZnCO_3 + H_2SO_4 \rightarrow ZnSO_4 + H_2O + CO_2\uparrow$$

(ii) Reacting zinc oxide with sulphuric acid

$$ZnO + H_2SO_4 \rightarrow ZnSO_4 + H_2O$$

It crystallises out from aqueous solution as hepta hydrate.

Description

Zinc sulphate occurs as colourless crystals or as a white crystalline powder. It is odourless.

Identification

Zinc sulphate responds to all tests for zinc salt and for sulphate.

Purity

(1) **Free acid:** Weigh 0.25 g of Zinc Sulphate, dissolve in 5 ml of water, and add 1 drop of methyl orange TS. No red colour develops.

(2) **Heavy metals:** Not more than 10 µg/g as Pb.

(3) **Alkali metal and alkali-earth metals:** Not more than 0.50%.

(4) **Arsenic:** Not more than 4.0 µg/g as As_2O_3.

Assay

Weigh accurately about 0.4 g of Zinc Sulphate, add 100 ml of water, and dissolve while warming if necessary. Add 5 ml of ammonia - ammonium chloride buffer (pH 10.7), and titrate with 0.05 mol/lEDTA (indicator: 0.1 ml of eriochrome black T TS) until the color of the solution changes to blue. Calculate on the anhydrous basis.

1 ml of 0.05 mol/l EDTA $\cong$ 8.073 mg of $ZnSO_4$

Applications:

1. As topical astringent.
2. As wound healer and adjuvant for antimicrobials for treatment of wounds, ulcers, acne etc.

6.6 Iodine (I)

Atomic number: 53,   **Atomic mass:** 126.9045

Iodine is a bluish-black solid with a metallic lustre, appearing to sublimate into a noxious violet-pink gas. Melting at 113.7 °C (236.7 °F), it forms compounds with many elements but is less reactive than the other members of its group, the halogens, and has some metallic light reflectance.

Biological Significance

It is an essential micronutrient. Body normally has 20-30 mg of iodine and more than 75% is in the thyroid gland, rest is in the mammary gland, gastric mucosa, and blood. It's only function is related to thyroid hormones, Thyroxin (T4) and Triiodothyronine (T3) and is required for their biosynthesis.

Daily Requirement

150 micrograms per day.

Sources

Food sources of marine origin (seaweed), processed foods, iodized salt, fresh water, milk, meat, vegetables, cereals etc. Goitrogens occurring naturally in foods can cause goiter by blocking absorption or utilisation of iodine (cabbage, turnips, peanuts, soybeans).

Absorption and Excretion

Iodine is absorbed in the form of iodide and occurs both as free and protein-bound iodine in circulation. It is stored in the thyroid gland, where it is used for the synthesis of T3 and T4. The hormone is degraded in target cells and in the liver and the iodine is conserved and recycled if needed.

Excretion is primarily *via* urine and small amounts from bile are excreted in the faeces.

Deficiency

Iodine deficiency causes Goitre—enlargement of the thyroid gland. The deficiency may be absolute—in areas of deficiency, or relative—adolescence, pregnancy, lactation.

Goiters are more prevalent in women and with increased age iodine deficiency is the world's most prevalent cause of brain damage.

Serious iodine deficiency during pregnancy may result in stillbirths, abortions and cretinism. The less visible, more pervasive form of iron and iodine deficiency that lowers intellectual performance at home and school may have far greater global and economic impact.

Public Health problem of Iodine

Global prevalence of iodine deficiency is from 30% to <15%. Every year, 50 million children are born without the protection that iodine offers to the growing brain and body. About 18 million of those will suffer some significant degree of mental impairment. Iodine deficiency remains the single greatest cause of mental retardation. The one third of the world's people without protection by iodised salt are the most marginalized populations – economically, culturally and geographically.

Epidemiological Assessment

Assessment is done by following ways

- Checking the prevalence of goitre or neurological hypothyroidism, or cretinism.
- Urinary iodine excretion.
- Performing thyroid function tests.
- Neonatal hypothyroidism is a sensitive indicator of environmental iodine deficiency.
- Serum T4 is a more sensitive indicator among adults.

6.6.1 Official Iodine Compounds

Sodium iodide and Potassium iodide

1. Sodium Iodide : NaI : Molecular Weight 149.89.

Content

Should contain NLT 99% & NMT 101.5 % of NaI on dry basis.

Description

It is a white, crystalline solid and hygroscopic in nature. As expected it is highly soluble in water. But, unlike NaCl or NaBr it shows very good solubility in alcohols as well as acetone.

Preparation

By action of iodine on sodium hydroxide. First sodium iodate is formed which gets reduced with carbon to sodium iodide.

$$6\ NaOH + 3I_2\ \rightarrow\ 5NaI + NaIO_3 + 3H_2O$$

$$NaIO_3 + 3C\ \rightarrow\ NaI + 3CO\uparrow$$

Identification

Sodium iodide responds to all tests of sodium and iodide.

Purity

(1) Alkalinity: Dissolve 1 g in 10 ml water and add 0.15 ml of 0.1 N sulphuric acid and add 1 drop of phenolphthalein TS.

No red colour develops.

(2) Potassium: Solution of 1 g of sample in 2 ml of water yields no precipitate with 1 ml of sodium bitartrate TS.

(3) Heavy metals: Not more than 0.001% w/w.

(4) Nitrate, Nitrite and Ammonia: When solution heated with NaOH and aluminium wire no evolution as discernable. On testing with red litmus paper, it should not turn blue.

Assay

Weigh accurately about 0.5 g of NaI, add 10 ml of water, and dissolve while warming if necessary. Add 35 ml of HCl and titrate with 0.05M KIO_3 until dark brown solution is reduced to pale brown. Add 1 ml of amaranth TS and continue titration to yellow end point.

1 ml of 0.05 M KIO_3 $\cong$14.99 mg of NaI

Applications

1. As an expectorant.
2. As iodine supplement in deficiency and goiter.

Dose

03 to 05 g.

2. PotassiumIodide : KI : Molecular Weight : 166.0028

Content

Should contain NLT 99% & NMT 101.5 % of KI calculated with reference to the dried substance.

Description

It is a white, crystalline solid less hygroscopic than NaI. Aged and impure samples are yellow because of the slow oxidation of the salt to potassium carbonate and elemental iodine.

$$4 KI + 2 CO_2 + O_2 \rightarrow 2 K_2CO_3 + 2 I_2$$

It is very soluble in water, freely soluble in glycerol, soluble in alcohol.

Preparation

By action of iodine on potassium hydroxide. First potassium iodate is formed which gets reduced with carbon to sodium iodide.

$$6 KOH + 3I_2 \rightarrow 5KI + KIO_3 + 3H_2O$$

$$KIO_3 + 3C \rightarrow KI + 3CO\uparrow$$

Identification

Potassium iodide responds to all tests of potassium and iodide.

Purity

(1) **Appearance of solution:** Solution is clear and colourless.

(2) **Alkalinity:** To 12.5 ml of solution S add 0.1 ml of bromothymol blue solution R_1. Not more than 0.5 ml of 0.01 M hydrochloric acid is required to change the colour of the indicator. [S = Sample, R_1 = Reagent std.]

(3) **Iodates:** To 10 ml of solution S add 0.25 ml of iodide-free starch solution R and 0.2 ml of dilute sulphuric acid R and allow to stand protected from light for 2 min. No blue colour develops.

(4) **Sulphates:** 10 ml of solution S diluted to 15 ml with distilled water R complies with the limit test for sulphates (150 ppm).

(5) **Thiosulphates:** To 10 ml of solution S add 0.1 ml of starch solution R and 0.1 ml of 0.005 M iodine. A blue colour is produced.

(6) **Heavy metals:** 12 ml of solution S complies with limit test A for heavy metals (10 ppm). Prepare the standard using lead standard solution (1 ppm Pb) R.

(7) **Iron:** 5 ml of solution S diluted to 10 ml with water Rcomplies with the limit test for iron (20 ppm) (8) Loss on drying (2.2.32). Not more than 1.0 per cent, determined on 1.00 g of previously powdered substance bydrying in an oven at 100-105 C for 3 h.

Assay

Dissolve 1.500 g in water R and dilute to 100.0 ml withthe same solvent. To 20.0 ml of the solution add 40 ml ofhydrochloric acid R and titrate with 0.05 M potassiumiodate until the colour changes from red to yellow. Add5 ml of chloroform R and continue the titration, shakingvigorously, until the chloroform layer is decolourised.

1 ml of 0.05 M KIO_3 ≅ 16.60 mg of KaI

Applications
1. As an expectorant.
2. As iodine supplement in deficiency and goiter.

Dose
03 to 06g.

Question Bank

1. Explain the physiological role of Iodine.
2. Explain physiological role of copper as an essential and trace element.
3. Write short notes on -

   (a) Inorganic compounds as iron supplements.

   (b) Assay of ferrous sulphate.
4. What are essential and trace ions? Discuss the absorption, distribution and physiological role of iron.
5. Explain role of copper as a trace element and also give details about its compounds. Explain zinc element and also give details about its compounds.
6. Explain iodine and also give details about its compounds.
7. What is the role of copper in metabolism?
8. Give the assay of ferric ammonium citrate.
9. Write the biochemical roles of following essential and trace elements in short   (any 2)

   (a) Iron, (b) Copper, (c) Zinc , (d) Iodine.
10 Short notes on any 3

   (a) Ferric Chloride, (b) Iron-Sorbitex Injection, (c) Sodium iodide (d) Zinc sulphate (e) Copper sulphate.
11. Explain the reactions involved in the assay of potassium iodide.
12. Discuss role of zinc and its salts as essential and trace ion.
13. Discuss role of iron in body. Describe briefly official preparations of iron.
14. Discuss the preparation and reactions involved to make Ferric ammonium citrate

Chapter 7...

Topical Agents

Contents ...

7.1   Introduction

7.2   Protectives

7.3   Antimicrobials and Astringents

    7.3.1   Antimicrobial Agents

    7.3.2   Astringents

•   Question Bank

7.1 Introduction

The term 'topical' means pertaining to a particular spot.

Topical agents are the compounds that act locally on the body surfaces i.e., skin and mucous membranes. They act mainly by physical or mechanical means. Their effects are seen primarily on the surfaces to which they are applied.

Topical application of these drugs may extend to such body cavities that are open to the outside. e.g., oral, vaginal and colonic cavities.

Topical agents may produce a variety of effects such as adsorbent, astringent or protective. Some topical agents may exhibit antimicrobial and astringent activities.

Classification of Topical Agents –

A.   Protective agents.

B.   Antimicrobial and astringent compounds.

7.2 Protectives

Protectives are substances which may be applied to the skin to protect certain areas from irritation, usually of mechanical origin. e.g., dusting powders like zinc stearate, zinc oxide etc.

These are generally insoluble and chemically inert substances, which are practically non-toxic and cover skin or mucous membrane from possible irritants. They act by physically blocking the pores and forming a protective layer on the surface of the skin or tissue.

There are some chemically inert substances which tend to adsorb dissolved or suspended particles of gases or toxins. Such substances are known as **adsorbents**. They are mainly used internally to prevent the irritating and undesirable action on mucous.

Adsorbents should not be applied to the abraded skin because of the possibility of enhancing the systemic absorption.

The action shown by protectives is known as mechanical protection. Protection from the external environment is due to the formation of a film or coat or a layer on the skin. The materials in the form of adhesive tapes, bandages, cream or pastes etc. are used for external applications.

1. Talc

Molecular Formula : $Mg_3SiO_{10}(OH)_2$ **Molecular Weight :** 379.26

Preparation

Talc is obtained by purifying native talc by boiling the finely powdered talc with dilute HCl and then washing the insoluble talc thoroughly with water until it becomes free from acid. Hydrochloric acid treatment is given for the removal of iron and other impurities such as Al_2O_3, CaO and Fe_2O_3.

Properties

Purified talc occurs as a very fine, white or greyish white powder. It is odourless and tasteless. It is free from grittiness and readily adheres to skin. Its solution is neutral to litmus. It is practically insoluble in water and dilute solutions of acids and alkalies. It has very low adsorptive property. It can be used as filtering aid, as it will not adsorb important constituents.

Storage

It is stored in tightly closed container and protected from moisture.

Uses

1. Talc is used as a dusting powder in cosmetic preparations.
2. It is generally used along with starch, zinc oxide and small amounts of boric acid.
3. It is perfumed or medicated.
4. It is also used as a filtering medium for clarifying liquids.
5. It is used as a lubricant for tablet granules but, recently magnesium stearate has replaced talc because of its better lubricating properties.

2. Zinc Oxide

Molecular Formula : ZnO,   **Molecular Weight :** 81.4

Zinc oxide contains not less than 99.0% and not more than 100.5 % of ZnO, calculated on the ignited basis

Preparation

ZnO is prepared in two ways :

(a) On large scale ZnO is obtained by heating metallic zinc, upto a high temperature in a current of air. The metal vapour burns to form the oxide, which is collected as a fine white powder.

$$2\ Zn + O_2 \xrightarrow{\Delta} 2\ ZnO$$

(b) The medicinal grade of zinc oxide is obtained from zinc sulphate. A solution of zinc sulphate is added to a boiling solution of sodium carbonate. The precipitated zinc carbonate is collected which is washed until it becomes free from sulphate. Now it is dried and ignited. Water and CO_2 are released leaving behind ZnO.

$$ZnSO_4 + Na_2CO_3 \longrightarrow ZnCO_3 + Na_2SO_4$$

$$ZnCO_3 \xrightarrow{\Delta} ZnO + CO_2\uparrow$$

Properties

It occurs as soft, white or faintly white, very fine powder, free from grittiness. It is odourless and tasteless, when exposed to air, it slowly absorbs carbon dioxide from the air. It is insoluble in water and alcohol.

As zinc oxide is amphoteric, it is soluble in solution of alkali hydroxide as well as, dilute mineral acids.

Storage

It is stored in a tightly closed container, protected from moisture.

Assay

It is assayed by acidimetric back titration method. An accurately weighed amount of about 1.5 g of sample is made to dissolve in 50 ml of 1 N sulphuric acid. To it 2.5 g of ammonium chloride is added and the excess of acid is titrated with 1 N sodium hydroxide employing methyl orange as an indicator.

Each ml of $1NH_2SO_4 \cong 0.04068$ m of ZnO

Uses

1. It acts as a mild antiseptic and as an astringent in the form of ointment or dusting powder which are officially approved for use in various pharmacopoeials.

2. It is widely used in the treatment of skin disease.

3. It is employed topically in the treatment of ringworm and psoriasis.

4. It is also used in the manufacture of adhesive tapes and bandages.

5. Dentists used it as a dental cement and for temporary fillings.

3. Calamine

Molecular Formula : Fe_2O_4Zn **Molecular Weight :** 241.06

Calamine is zinc oxide having a small amount of ferric oxide. It is cosmetically better accepted than zinc oxide.

Preparation

Zinc oxide needed for calamine is obtained by heating zinc carbonate. Zinc oxide is then mixed with ferric oxide (upto 1.0%) thoroughly to prepare calamine.

$$ZnCO_3 \xrightarrow{\Delta} ZnO + CO_2\uparrow$$

Properties

It is an odourless, tasteless pink powder. It passes through a seive No. 100. It is almost insoluble in water but, completely soluble in mineral acids.

Storage

It is stored in a closed container protected from light and moisture.

Assay

An ignited and cooled sample is first weighed. It is then dissolved in 50 ml of 1 N sulphuric acid and filtered. The residue is washed with hot water till it is free of any trace of acids, filtrate and washings are combined.

To this ammonium chloride is added and titrated with 1 N sodium hydroxide using methyl orange as an indicator. Ammonium chloride is added to prevent precipitation of zinc hydroxide during titration. Precipitation of zinc hydroxide results in a poorly defined end point.

Each ml of 1N $H_2SO_4 \cong 0.04068$ gm of ZnO

Uses

1. It is used as a mild astringent, antiseptic and protectant for the skin.
2. It has a soothing effect in eczema.
3. It is used for soothing purposes in ointments and lotions used to treat sun burns, etc.

4. Zinc Stearate

   Molecular Formula ($[CH_3(CH_2)_{16}CO_2]Zn$),   **Molecular Weight :** 632.34

   Zinc stearate contains not less than 10.0% and not more than 12.0% of zinc.

Preparation

Zinc stearate is obtained by adding zinc sulphate solution to a solution of sodium stearate and washing the precipitate with water until it is completely free of sulphate.

The commercial stearic acid, which is used for preparing sodium stearate, always contains different proportions of palmitic acid. Stearic acid is obtained by the hydrolysis of fats and is subjected to partial purification for separating other fatty acids of low melting points, which are produced along with stearic acid.

$$2C_{17}H_{35}COONa + ZnSO_4 \rightarrow (C_{17}H_{35}COO)_2Zn + Na_2SO_4$$

   Sodium stearate   Zinc stearate

      (soap)

Properties

It is a white, fine amorphous powder free from grittiness. It has a faint characteristic odour. It is unctuous to touch and adheres to skin readily. It is insoluble in water, alcohol and ether.

Assay

Zinc stearate is assayed by complexometric, as well as, acidimetric back titration method. An accurate weighed (1.0 g) sample is gently boiled with 50.0 ml of 0.1 N H_2SO_4. The clear oily layer of stearic acid separates out. The remaining solution is filtered and washed thoroughly with water until last washing is not acidic to litmus. A strong ammonia - ammonium chloride solution (15.0 ml) is added to the combined filtrate and washings. Thereafter, 0.2 ml of erichrome black T indicator is added. The solution is heated to about 40°C and titrated with 0.05 M disodium EDTA until deep blue colour appears.

Each ml of 0.05 M dissodium EDTA $\cong 0.004068$ gm of ZnO

Uses

1. It acts as a mild astringent and has antimicrobial properties.
2. It is used in dermatology for its protective properties and also in water repellent ointments and dusting powders.
3. However, its use as a routine dusting powder for children should be discouraged as its inhalation causes pulmonary inflammation.
4. Because of its lubricant action it is used as lubricant in tableting.

5. Titanium Dioxide

Molecular Formula : TiO_2,   **Molecular Weight :** 79.90

It contains not less than 98% TiO_2, calculated with reference to the dried substance.

Preparation

It is obtained from natural sample of ilmenite or form rutile. The ore is heated with conc. sulphuric acid until sulphates of iron and titanium are dissolved in water.The precipitate of titanium dioxide is obtained by hydrolysis.

Properties

It occurs as a white or almost white fluffy powder, odourless and tasteless. It is practically insoluble in water and in dilute mineral acids. It dissolves slowly in hot sulphuric acid.

It becomes soluble in water when fused with alkali hydroxides, carbonates or bisulphates.

Storage

It is stored in tightly closed containers.

Assay

It is assayed by complexometric sodium edetate back titration method.

Weighed accurately (0.3 gm) sample is dissolved by heating a mixture of 20 ml of sulphuric acid and 8.0 gm of ammonium sulphate. The solution is diluted to 100 ml with water and boiled with continuous stirring. After cooling to room temperature the solution is filtered. The residue is washed several times with 10 ml of water. A strong ammonia solution (10 ml) is added to the combined filtrate and washings and then diluted to 200 ml with water. To 50 ml of resulting solution, 100 ml of water and 4 ml of strong H_2O_2 solution is added. After adding 50 ml of 0.05 M disodium EDTA the solution is allowed to stand for 5 minutes. The pH of solution is adjusted to 5.0 with NaOH solution and by adding 5.0 g of hexamine. The resulting solution is titrated with 0.05 M $ZnCl_2$ using xylenol orange solution as an indicator.

Each ml of 0.05 M disodium EDTA $\cong$ 0.003995 gm of TiO_2

Uses

1. Titanium dioxide is a good topical protective.

2. The protective action is due to opacity of the compound.

3. It protects the skin from harmful ultraviolet radiation and hence is commonly employed in skin protective creams, pastes etc.

4. Due to white colour it is used in cosmetic preparations and in paints.

6. **Aluminium Compounds : Aluminium chloride, Aluminium sulphate**

   Aluminium Chloride : Molecular Formula : $AlCl_3.6H_2O$,   **Molecular Weight :** 241.43

   It contains not less than 95% of $AlCl_3.6H_2O$

Preparation

It may be prepared by heating metallic aluminium in a current of chlorine dissolving the product in water and then crystallising it.

$$2Al + 3Cl_2 \longrightarrow 2AlCl_3$$

Properties

It forms white-deliquescent, crystalline powder. It has a sweet astringent taste and a mild odour. It is highly soluble in water and in alcohol. In non-polar solvents it exists as a dimer, Al_2Cl_6.

Uses

1. The aqueous solution of the compound in (10.25% w/v) is used as a mild antiseptic and astringent.

2. Due to tissue irritation and staining of clothes, the compound is not used routinely.

Aluminium Sulphate

Molecular Formula : $Al_2(SO_4)_3. H_2O$,   **Molecular Weight :** 342.14

It should have not less than 51.0% and not more than 59.0% of $Al_2(SO_4)_3$.

Preparation

It may be prepared by interaction of freshly precipitated aluminium hydroxide with equivalent quantity of sulphuric acid. After the reaction is over, the resultant solution is concentrated and allowed to crystallise. The crystals are filtered and dried.

$$2Al(OH)_2 + 3H_2SO_4 \rightarrow Al_2(SO_4)_3$$

Properties

Aluminium sulphate forms white crystalline powder. It is odourless and has sweet astringent taste. It is highly soluble in water, insoluble in alcohol. The crystalline salt dehydrates on heating at 250°.

Assay

Its assay is based upon the complexometric back titration method. A known weight of sample is dissolved in 1N hydrochloric acid, and excess disodium edetate is added and the solution is neutralised using methyl orange as indicator. It is then heated and titrated with standard lead nitrate solution using xylenol orange as an indicator.

Uses

1. It is used as liquid deodorant in its solution form.
2. It is used as an antiperspirant, as 10 - 15% w/v aluminium sulphate in form of a cream.
3. A 5.25 % w/v solution is used topically.
4. A 10% w/v solution is used for disinfection of dental cavities.

7.3 Antimicrobials and Astringents

7.3.1 Antimicrobial Agents

These are the chemicals whose preparations help in reducing or preventing infection due to microbes. Several terms employed in describing antimicrobial activity are as given below.

1. **Antiseptics :** These are substances that are able to kill or prevent the growth of micro-organisms. This term is specific for preparations which are to be applied to living tissues.
2. **Disinfectants :** These are the substances that prevent infection by the destruction of pathogenic micro-organisms.
3. **Germicides :** These are substances which kill micro-organisms.
4. **Bacteriostatics :** These are substances which primarily function by inhibiting the growth of bacteria. Thus, bacteriostatic drugs or agents do not kill, but arrest the growth of bacteria.
5. **Sterilization :** This refers to the use of a disinfectant or any other procedure to render an object completely free of micro-organisms.

Mechanism of Action

Antimicrobial action involve either of the following three mechanisms –

1. Oxidation.
2. Halogenation.
3. Protein binding or precipitation.

(1) Oxidation Mechanism : Compounds acting by this mechanism belong to class of oxygen liberating compounds like peroxides and peroxyacids, permanganate and certain oxo-halogen anions.

These anti-infective agents bring about oxidation of active functional groups present in proteins or enzymes vital to the growth or survival of micro organisms. This causes a change in the conformation of the proteins and thereby alter their function. e.g., free sulphydryl group has been essential for functioning of a variety of proteins and enzymes. This free nature of sulpyhydryl group gets destroyed by oxidation resulting into the formation of a disulfide bond.

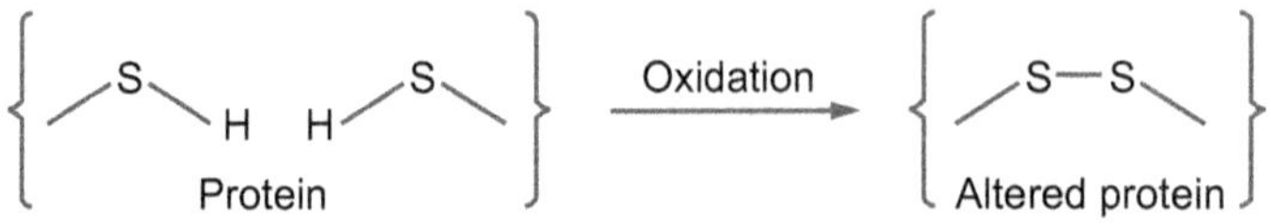

$$\left\{ \ce{S-H} \quad \ce{H-S} \right\}_{\text{Protein}} \xrightarrow{\text{Oxidation}} \left\{ \ce{S-S} \right\}_{\text{Altered protein}}$$

Fig. 7.1 : Mechanism of oxidation of proteins

(2) Halogenation Mechanisms : Compounds which are able to liberate chlorine or hypochlorite or iodine act by this mechanism. This category of agents act on peptide linkage and alter its potential and property. The destruction of specific function of protein cause death of micro organism.

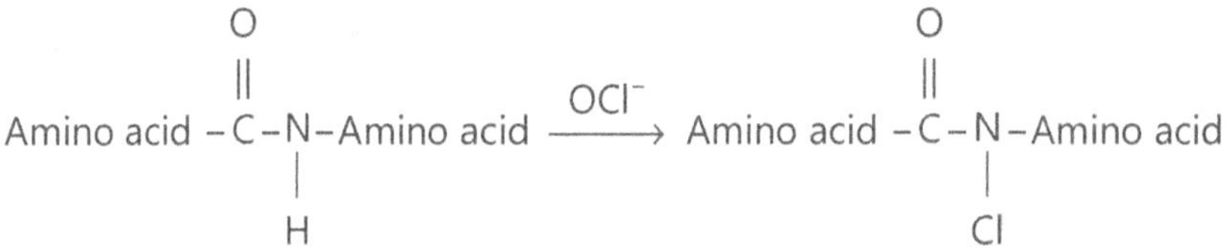

$$\underset{\text{Protein structure}}{\text{Amino acid} - \overset{\displaystyle O}{\overset{\|}{C}} - \underset{|}{\underset{H}{N}} - \text{Amino acid}} \xrightarrow{\text{OCl}^-} \underset{\text{Altered protein}}{\text{Amino acid} - \overset{\displaystyle O}{\overset{\|}{C}} - \underset{|}{\underset{Cl}{N}} - \text{Amino acid}}$$

Most of the enzymes are proteineous in nature. A protein molecule is composed of a variety of amino acids bound by a peptide (–CONH–) linkage. As hypochlorides (OCl⁻) are found to chlorinate peptide linkage, antiseptics having hypochlorite functional group exert their antimicrobial activity by chlorination of peptide linkage in protein molecules.

The substitution of chlorine atom in place of nitrogen of the peptide linkage causes a change in H-bonding forces responsible for proper orientation of the protein molecule. Hence, the functions of protein cannot be carried out.

(3) Protein Binding or Precipitation : Many metal ions exhibit protein binding or protein precipitation properties.

The interaction of metal ions with protein is non-specific and at sufficient concentrations will react with host, as well as, microbial proteins.

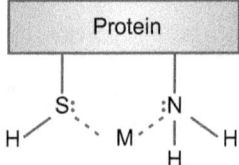

Fig. 7.2 : Mechanism of protein precipitation

Certain metals (e.g., mercury, arsenic and antimony) show some enzyme specificity and form strong covalent bonds with particular enzyme systems.

7.3.2 Astringents

These are the compounds which bring about protein precipitation.

They are usually applied to damaged skin topically or to the mucous membrane of the GIT including the mouth.

Mechanism of Action :

Due to their protein precipitant action, astringents are able to reduce cell permeability. Astringents are also known to inhibit the transcapillary movement of plasma proteins. This helps to reduce local edema and inflammation. Mucous secretion is also found to get reduced.

When applied topically, astringents in low concentrations are found to stimulate growth of a new tissue. While in high concentration, astringents bring about corrosive effect on tissue. The protein precipitation is brought about by astringent in the presence of metallic ions having large charge radius ratio or strong electrostatic fields.

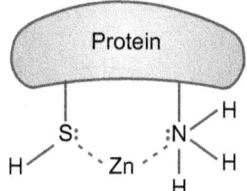

Fig. 7.3 : Mechanism of astringent action

The metal would form complex with various polar groups present on the protein or an enzyme. This complexation of important functional groups at the active site of protein or an enzyme causes a drastic change in the properties of the protein.

In general, astringent compounds do exhibit :

(i) **styptic action :** Stopping of bleeding by coagulation of blood and constriction of small capillaries;

(ii) **anti-inflammatory action :** By decreasing the supply of blood to the tissues;

(iii) **anti-perspirant action :** By decreasing secretion of perspiration by reducing pore size of skin and;

(iv) **antimicrobial action :** By protein precipitation mechanism.

Astringents have other uses also –

1. They are used to treat diarrhoea.
2. They also possess deodorant properties.
3. They decrease sweating and make the skin tougher.
4. They promote healing process.

1. **Hydrogen Peroxide**

   Molecular Formula : H_2O_2 **Molecular Weight :** 34.016

   It has not less than 6% w/w of H_2O_2 which corresponds to about 20 times its volume of available oxygen.

Preparation

Hydrogen peroxide is obtained by two ways :

1. It is obtained by adding a thick paste of barium peroxide in ice cold water to a calculated quantity of ice cold dilute sulphuric acid. The insoluble barium sulphate is filtered out.

$$BaO_2 + H_2SO_4 \longrightarrow BaSO_4\downarrow + H_2O_2$$

2. H_2O_2 is also obtained by treating sodium peroxide with dil. H_2SO_4 at low temperature. Sodium sulphate crystallises out and H_2O_2 is distilled under 10 mm pressure.

$$Na_2O_2 + H_2SO_4 \longrightarrow Na_2SO_4 + H_2O_2$$

Properties

Hydrogen peroxide is a colourless and odourless liquid having a slightly acidic taste. The solution decomposes when it comes in contact with oxidisable matter or when made alkaline.

$$2H_2O_2 \longrightarrow 2H_2O + O_2$$

The decomposition is promoted by a catalyst such as Cu, Fe, Mn etc. whereas small quantity of acids such as H_2SO_4, H_3PO_4 and alcohol, if added, retard decomposition of H_2O_2. Therefore, they act as negative catalysts and are used as preservatives or stabilisers in commercial preparations.

Hydrogen peroxide is a strong oxidising agent and is miscible in water from which it can be extracted with solvent ether.

Storage

It is preserved in a light resistant container with a stopper made of glass or plastic resistant to hydrogen peroxide. It is kept in a dark, and cool place.

Assay

It is carried out by permanganate method in which 10 ml of the sample is diluted to 250 ml in a volumetric flask with purified water. To 25 ml of this solution 10 ml of 5 N sulphuric acid is added. Then the contents are titrated with 0.1 N KMnO$_4$ solution, until a faint pink colour is obtained.

$$2\,KMnO_4 + 3H_2SO_4 + 5H_2SO_4 \longrightarrow K_2SO_4 + 8H_2O + 5O_2 + 2MnSO_4$$

Each ml of 0.1 N KMnO$_4$ $\cong$ 0.001701 gm of H$_2$O$_2$

Note : H_2O_2 and $KMnO_4$ both are oxidising agents. These two oxidising agents reduce one another with the evolution of gaseous oxygen. H_2O_2 reduces $KMnO_4$ solution and causes its decolouration. At the end point, excess drop of $KMnO_4$ gives pink colour. $KMnO_4$ itself acts as an indicator.

Uses

1. It is a strong oxidising agent.
2. It is used for bleaching.
3. It acts as an antiseptic and a germicide and hence it is used for cleaning cuts and wounds.

4. It is an effective antidote for phosphorus and cyanide poisoning.

5. It also finds use for cleaning ears and during removal of surgical dressings.

2. Sodium Perborate

Molecular Formula : $NaBO_3 \cdot 4H_2O$,   **Molecular Weight :** 153.9

Sodium perborate has not less than 96% and not more than 103% $NaBO_3.4H_2O$.

Preparation

Sodium perborate is prepared by adding sodium hydroxide and double the theoretical quantity of hydrogen peroxide to a saturated solution of borate.

$$Na_2B_4O_7 + 2NaOH + 4H_2O_2 \longrightarrow 4NaBO_3 + 5H_2O$$

It is also prepared by passing carbon dioxide in a solution obtained by adding sodium peroxide to a solution of boric acid.

Properties

Sodium perborate is available in the form of white granules or powder having a saline taste. It is soluble in 40 parts of water. Its solubility is also increased by the presence of magnesium or ammonium sulphate.

Storage

It is preserved in tight containers and kept in a cool place.

Assay

0.3 g of sodium perborate is weighed accurately and dissolved in 50 ml water. The solution is then acidified with 10 ml of dil. sulphuric acid and titrated with 0.1 N potassium permanganate.

$$NaBO_3.4H_2O \rightleftharpoons H_2O_2 + NaBO_2 + 3H_2O$$

$$5H_2O_2 + 2KMnO_4 + 3H_2SO_4 \longrightarrow 5O_2 + K_2SO_4 + 2MnSO_4 + 8H_2O$$

Use

Sodium perborate finds use as an oxidant and a local anti-infective and also as dentifrice and dusting powder.

3. Zinc Peroxide

Molecular Formula : ZnO_2 **Molecular Weight :** 97.39

Preparation

It is obtained by reacting zinc hydroxide with hydrogen peroxide.

$$Zn(OH)_2 + H_2O_2 \longrightarrow ZnO_2 + 2H_2O$$

Properties

It occurs as a white or slightly yellow powder.

Assay

It is assayed by titration with potassium permanganate (as for hydrogen peroxide) solution. It reduces $KMnO_4$ solution and causes its decolouration. At the end point, excess drops of $KMnO_4$ yield pink colour. Potassium permanganate itself acts as an indicator.

Use

It finds use for its protective astringent and mild antiseptic properties.

4. Potassium Permanganate

Molecular Formula : $KMnO_4$,   **Molecular Weight :** 158.0

It has not less than 99% w/w of $KMnO_4$.

Preparation

On a large scale, potassium permanganate is prepared by mixing a solution of KOH with powdered manganese oxide and potassium chlorate. The mixture is boiled and evaporated to yield the residue which is heated in iron pans until it has acquired a paste like consistency.

$$KOH + 3MnO_2 + KClO_3 \longrightarrow K_2MnO_4 + KCl + 3H_2O$$
Potassium
manganate

Potassium manganate so formed is extracted with boiling water and a current of chlorine, CO_2 or ozonised air is passed into the liquid until it gets converted to permanganate. The MnO_2 formed is removed continuously so as to prevent its breaking down to manganate.

$$6K_2MnO_4 + 3Cl_2 \longrightarrow 6KMnO_4 + 6KCl$$

When CO_2 is passed through the solution in place of chlorine, only two-third of manganate gets converted into $KMnO_4$. One third is converted into MnO_2.

$$3K_2MnO_4 + 2CO_2 \longrightarrow 2KMnO_4 + MnO_2 + 2K_2CO_3$$

The solution of $KMnO_4$ is drawn off from any precipitate of MnO_2 which is then concentrated and crystallised. The crystals are then centrifuged and dried.

Properties

Potassium permanganate occurs in the form of dark purple coloured monoclinic prisms, almost opaque having a blue metallic luster. It is odourless. It is soluble in 15 parts of water and 3.5 parts of boiling water. A solution of $KMnO_4$ has a sweetish, astringent taste. It acts as a powerful oxidising agent.

Storage

It is kept in tightly closed containers. It must be handled with care because an explosion may occur when it is brought in contact with readily oxidisable substances.

Assay

Its assay is based upon the oxidation - reduction reaction. Potassium permanganate is a strong oxidising agent and oxalic acid is a reducing agent. The reaction between $KMnO_4$ and oxalic acid tends to proceed slowly. Hence, warming at 70°C is required.

An accurately weighed amount of about 0.8 g of sample is dissolved in water. Then it is diluted with water to 250 ml. This solution is titrated with 25 ml of 0.1 N oxalic acid which is mixed with 25 ml of water and 5 ml of sulphuric acid. The temperature is maintained at about 70°C throughout the entire titration.

$$5H_2C_2O_4 + 2H_2O + 2KMnO_4 + 3H_2SO_4 \longrightarrow K_2SO_4 + 2MnSO_4 + 18H_2O + 10CO_2$$

Each ml of 0.1 N oxalic acid $\cong 0.00316$ gm of $KMnO_4$

Uses

1. It is used as an antiseptic in mouth wash.
2. As anti-infective it is regarded of immense value.
3. It is used in the treatment of urethritis.
4. As it is capable of oxidising some drugs and used as an antidote in case of poisonings by barbiturates, chloral hydrate, many alkaloids.
5. A solution of potassium permanganate can destroy poison and prevent its absorption. But it should not be kept in stomach for a long time.
6. In veterinary practice, it has been very commonly used as an antiseptic.

5. Sodium Hypochlorite

Molecular Formula : NaOCl,   **Molecular Weight :** 74.5

Preparation

Sodium hypochlorite is generally prepared by passing appropriate quantity of chlorine gas into a cold solution of sodium hydroxide or sodium carbonate.

$$2NaOH + Cl_2 \longrightarrow NaOCl + NaCl + H_2O$$
$$\text{Sodium}$$
$$\text{hypochlorite}$$

The solution is made to keep cool during the passage of chlorine gas, otherwise chlorate instead of hypochlorite is formed.

Properties

Sodium hypochlorite is a pale-greenish liquid having smell of chlorine. The solution is affected by light. It turns red litmus blue and then bleaches it.

Storage

Sodium hypochlorite being unstable, the solution is stored in a tight, light-resistant containers and kept at cool place.

Assay

A weighed amount of sample is treated with acetic acid and potassium iodide. The iodine liberated is made to titrate with standard sodium thiosulphate solution using starch as an indicator.

Uses

1. The solution of sodium hypochlorite is too strong to be used on tissues due to its caustic (alkalinity) and oxidising action.
2. The dilute solution is primarily used for disinfectant and antibacterial action.

6. Iodine Solution

Molecular Formula : I_2,   **Atomic Weight :** 126.9

Iodine solution does not have less than 99.5% of I_2.

Preparation

Iodine is manufactured by extracting kalp (seaweed's ash) with water. The solution is concentrated when the sulphate and chloride of sodium and potassium are crystallised out, leaving freely soluble sodium and potassium iodides in the mother liquor. Sulphuric acid is added to the mother liquor and sulphur, which gets liberated from small amount of thiosulphate and sulphide, is allowed to settle down. The mother liquor is decanted, and to this MnO_2 is then added and the iodine distils over.

$$2NaI + 3H_2SO_4 + MnO_2 \longrightarrow MnSO_4 + 2NaHSO_4 + I_2 + 2H_2O$$

Properties

Iodine is in the form of heavy, bluish-black, rhombic prism or plate having a metallic lustre. It has a peculiar odour and is volatile at ordinary temperature. At higher temperature it melts. It is insoluble in water but soluble in alcohol. It is freely soluble in chloroform and solvent ether and in aqueous solution of iodides.

Storage

It is preserved in glass stoppered, amber coloured bottles and kept in a cool place.

Assay

It may be assayed by involving the oxidation - reduction titration method.

About 0.5 gm of iodine is first dissolved in a solution of 1 gm of potassium iodide (1 gm potassium iodide in 5 ml water) in an iodine flask. It is diluted with 50 ml of water and acidified with 1 ml of acetic acid. The resulting solution is titrated with standard sodium thiosulphate, using starch solution as an indicator.

$$2Na_2S_2O_3 + I_2 \longrightarrow Na_2S_4O_6 + 2NaI$$

Each ml of 0.1 N sodium thiosulphate $\cong 0.01269$ gm of I_2

Uses

1. Iodine is used in medicine mainly as a counter irritant and disinfectant.
2. It is used as a local germicide.
3. Elemental iodine can exert its action when used externally.
4. In the treatment of goitre iodine is supplied to the body either in the elemental form or in the form of sodium or potassium iodide.

7. Aqueous Iodine Solution

It has 5.0% w/v of iodine and 10% w/v of KI.

Composition

Iodine	50 g
KI	100 g
Purified water sufficient to produce	1000 ml

Preparation

KI and I are first dissolved in 100 ml of water with trituration or shaking. Then the volume is made up to 1000 ml by adding sufficient volume of purified water.

Properties

It is a transparent, brown liquid, having the smell of iodine.

Assay

The assay of aqueous iodine solution is carried out for iodine and potassium iodide. 25 ml of the aqueous iodine solution is first diluted to 100 ml with water and this diluted solution is used for assay.

Uses

1. It acts as a good source of iodine and is taken internally.
2. It possesses germicidal and fungicidal properties.

(a) Weak Iodine Solution

Iodine tincture is having 2% w/v of iodine and 2.5% w/v of KI.

Preparation

Potassium iodide and iodine are first dissolved in sufficient alcohol. The volume is then made upto 1000 ml by adding more 50% alcohol.

Properties

These are the same as those described under aqueous iodine solution.

Assay

For iodine 10 ml of solution is first diluted with 20 ml of water. Then it is titrated with 0.1 N sodium thiosulphate using starch solution as an indicator.

Use

It is a well known and popular antiseptic, which is applied on cuts and wounds.

(b) Strong Iodine Solution

It has 10% of iodine and 6% w/v of potassium iodide.

Preparation

Potassium iodide and iodine are first dissolved in purified water, the sufficient amount of alcohol is added to make up the volume to 1000 ml.

Properties

These are the same as described under aqueous iodine solution.

Use

It is used as an antiseptic.

8. **Boric Acid**

Molecular Formula : H_3BO_3,   **Molecular Weight :** 61.83

It has not less than 99.5% of H_3BO_3.

Preparation

In the laboratory, boric acid is obtained by adding a mixture of conc. H_2SO_4 and water to a boiling solution of borax.

$$Na_2B_4O_7 + H_2SO_4 + 5H_2O \longrightarrow Na_2SO_4 + 4H_3BO_3$$

The solution is filtered and kept aside for crystallisation. The crystals of boric acid are separated and then washed until they become free from sulphate ions. Finally, they are dried at room temperature.

Properties

Boric acid is a solid which is available in three forms :

1. Colourless, odourless pearly scales.
2. Six-sided triclinic crystals.
3. White odourless powder.

It is odourless with slightly acidic and bitter taste and unctuous touch.

It is stable in air, and has a density of 1.46. Boric acid is a weak acid.

Assay

It is assayed by a titrimetric methods. An accurately weighed quantity of boric acid is dissolved in a mixture of 50 ml of water, and 100 ml glycerine previously neutralised to phenolphthalein. Now this solution is titrated with 1 N NaOH using phenolphthalein as an indicator.

Each ml of 1 N NaOH $\cong 0.06183$ gm of H_3BO_3

Uses

1. It is used as a local anti-infective agent.
2. It is used in dusting powders, local antiseptic creams, ointments, lotions etc. applied to skin or mucous or eye.
3. Aqueous solutions have been used as mouth wash, eye lotions, skin lotions.
4. It possesses weak bacteriostatic and fungistatic action.

Properties

Its solution is not an irritant and is hence used for washing the eyes.

It is used in dusting powders after trituration with some other inert materials.

It is toxic when taken internally and is absorbed from gastro-intestinal tract and from broken skin.

Boric acid can be very dangerous if ingested. Therefore, its container should bear the warning *"Not for internal use".*

9. Selenium Sulphide

Molecular Formula : SeS_2,   **Molecular Weight :** 143.01

It has between 52 - 55% of selenium.

Preparation

Selenium disulphide may be prepared by passing hydrogen sulphide gas into selenious acid or by adding selenious acid to a saturated solution of hydrogen sulphide. The precipitate is filtered and dried.

$$H_2SeO_3 + 2H_2S \longrightarrow SeS_2\downarrow + 3H_2O$$

It dissolves in nitric acid and forms selenious acid and sulphuric acid.

$$SeS_2 + 16\,HNO_3 \longrightarrow H_2SeO_3 + 2H_2SO_4$$

The compound is highly toxic and should not be allowed to enter in the eyes.

Properties

It is a bright orange powder having faint sulphide odour. It is practically insoluble in water, alcohol and organic solvents.

Assay

It may be assayed by oxidation - reduction titration. It is an iodometric titration, where the liberated iodine is titrated with sodium thiosulphate.

Weight 0.1 gm of selenium sulphide and solubilise in 25 ml of fuming nitric acid with the help of heat. After cooling, it is diluted to 100 ml with water. To 25 ml of resulting solution, 10 ml of potassium iodide and 10 ml chloroform are added. This solution is immediately titrated with 0.02 N sodium thiosulphate until aqueous layer attains pale straw colour. Stopper the flask and shake vigorously for 30 seconds. Add 0.1 ml starch mucilage as an indicator and continue the titration until blue colour disappears from the aqueous layer.

Each ml of 0.02 N sodium thiosulphate $\cong$ 0.01974 gm of selenium

Uses

1. It is used topically as an anti-dandruff in shampoos.
2. Selenium sulphide is added to shampoos in 1 - 2.5 % as antiseborrhic.
3. It should not be administered internally.

10. Zinc Sulphate

Molecular Formula : $ZnSO_4.7H_2O$,   **Molecular Weight :** 287.6

It does not have less than 55.6% and not more than 61% of $ZnSO_4$.

Preparation

It is obtained by heating zinc blende (zinc sulphide) in the presence of air under specific conditions. The heated mass is dissolved in hot water, filtered and solution is concentrated for crystallisation.

$$ZnS + 2O_2 \longrightarrow ZnSO_4$$

Properties

It forms colourless transparent crystals, prisms or needles, or as a granular, crystalline powder. It is odourless with an astringent and metallic taste. It is very soluble in water and glycerine but insoluble in alcohol.

Storage

It is preserved in well closed containers in a cool place.

Assay

It is assayed gravimetrically. An accurately weighed amount of substance of about 1 gm is dissolved in 100 ml of water, then this solution is heated to about 90°C. To the hot solution, with constant stirring, a solution of sodium carbonate is added until there occurs, complete precipitation of zinc carbonate. Care should be taken not to add an excess of sodium carbonate. The precipitated zinc carbonate solution is boiled for a few minutes, filtered through gooch crucible, which is washed with hot water, until it is free from alkali. The residue is dried, ignited, and weighed.

Each gm of residue $\cong 1.984$ gm of $ZnSO_4$

Uses

1. When used internally, zinc sulphate acts as an emetic acting upon the vomiting reflex.
2. Its action is very rapid and does not cause local irritation to gastric mucosa.
3. Externally, it is used in solution and powders as an astringent.
4. For ophthalmic purpose 0.25% w/v solution is employed.
5. The aqueous solution of zinc sulphate is also employed for protein precipitation. However, the eye solutions, if prepared without a borate buffer, are acidic.

Question Bank

1. What are topical agents ? Classify topical agents.
2. What are protective adsorbents ? What is their mode of action ?
3. Define the terms : (a) Astringent, (b) Bactericidal, (c) Disinfectant.
4. Write a notes on :
   (a) Boric acid   (b) Potassium permanganate
   (c) Iodine solution   (d) Selenium sulphide
   (e) Hydrogen peroxide.
5. Write a note on iodine preparations as topical agents.
6. Describe with principle and reaction involved in hydrogen peroxide assay.
7. Explain the properties, uses and method of assay of talc and zinc oxide.
8. Classify topical agents on the basis of their action with suitable examples.
9. Comment on assay of potassium permanganate.
10. Write a short note on astringents.
11. Discuss the different mechanism of action for antimicrobial agents with suitable figures.

✍ ✍ ✍

Chapter **8**...

Dental Products

Contents ...

8.1   Definition
    8.1.1   Abrasives
    8.1.2   Cleaning Agents or Dentifrices
    8.1.3   Dental Caries and Anticaries Agents
8.2   Caries Prevention
    8.2.1   Fluoride
    8.2.2   Polishing Agents
    8.2.3   Desensitising Agents
    8.2.4   Anti-calculus Agents
    8.2.5   Whitening Agents
    8.2.6   Pumice
8.3   Preparation and Assay of Some Important Anti-caries Agents
•   Question Bank

8.1 Definition

Dental products are mainly used for treating and/or cleaning the teeth.

Dentifrice: Dentrifice can be defined as any substance specially prepared for cleaning the surfaces of teeth. The dental products are mainly used in the form of tooth paste, transparent tooth paste, mouth wash, tooth cleaning powder, gel, cleaning agents for dentures, chewing gum etc.

Some important definitions are mentioned below-

(a) **Abrasive:** Solid materials that are added to dentifrices to facilitate mechanical removal of dental plaque, debris, and stain from tooth surfaces.

(b) **Anticaries drug:** A drug that aids in the prevention and prophylactic treatment of dental cavities (decay, caries).

(c) **Dental caries:** A disease of calcified tissues of teeth characterised by demineralisation of the inorganic portion and destruction of the organic matrix.

(d) **Dentifrice:** An abrasive-containing dosage form (gel, paste, or powder) for delivering an anticaries drug to the teeth.

(e) **Fluoride:** The inorganic form of the chemical element fluorine in combination with other elements.

(f) **Fluoride ion:** The negatively charged atom of the chemical element fluorine.

8.1.1 Abrasives

An abrasive is a substance that is used for abrading, grinding or polishing. The degree of abrasivity depends on the hardness of the abrasive, the morphology of the particles and on the concentration of abrasive in the paste. The abrasives found in toothpastes are often not as hard as the enamel, but as hard as or harder than the dentine. Abrasives are most often found as crystals; small and smooth particles are preferred to avoid tooth wear. Transparent toothpastes, commonly called gel toothpastes, are obtained by mixing certain abrasives. The amount and type of abrasive in toothpaste contributes to give the toothpaste its creamy consistency. The abrasive effect is measured in the RDA (Radioactive Dentine Abrasion) scale, ranging from 40-80 in most toothpastes. Hydrated silica is a common abrasive in dentifrices; alumina and calcium carbonate may also be used.

8.1.2 Cleaning Agent or Dentifrices

It is a material, a powder or paste used for cleaning of teeth which can be applied with brush. Cleaning property depends on the rubbing force used.

Drawback: Cannot clean surface inside cavities and crevices between teeth. Dentifrices with useful substances are known as medicated dentifrices. Flavours and colours are used to improve acceptance. A good cleaning agent removes the stains from teeth. Examples of cleaning agents or dentifrices are calcium phosphate dibasic and tribasic calcium phosphate, calcium carbonate and sodium metaphosphate

8.1.3 Dental Caries and Anticaries Agents

Dental caries is a pathologic process of microbial etiology that results in localised destruction of tooth tissues. The process of tooth destruction involves dissolution of the mineral phase, consisting primarily of hydroxyapatite crystals by organic acids produced by bacterial fermentation.

8.2 Caries Prevention

1. The prevention of dental caries is based on attempts to -
   (a) increase the resistance of the host (fluoride therapy, occlusal sealants, immunization).
   (b) lower the number of cariogenic microorganisms in contact with tooth (plaque control agents and antiplaque agents).
   (c) modify the substrate by selecting noncariogenic foods.
   (d) reduce the time that the microflora is provided with substrate by limiting the frequency of intake of fermentable substrate.
2. The formation of bacterial plaque also helps the decay process by forming pockets or crevices on the tooth surface in which the food particles can stick and be decayed by the bacteria. If plaque is not removed, it calcifies into calculus when calcium salt precipitates from the saliva. Brushing the teeth helps in removing the material from the tooth surface before it hardens into calculus.

3. Dental caries can be prevented and oral and dental hygiene can be maintained with the help of dentifrices. These are the products that enhance the removal of stain and dental plaque by the toothbrush.

4. The most accepted approach to prevent caries includes flossing and brushing accompanied by administration of fluoride either internally or topically to the teeth.

8.2.1 Fluoride

Fluorides obtained from food and water are very effective in prevention of dental caries.

Fluoridation: Fluoridation can be carried out by addition of fluoride to the water. However, high fluoride cause mottling of teeth, increased density of bone, gastric disturbance, muscular weakness, convulsions and heart failure.

Role of fluoride when salt or solution of fluoride is taken internally: Fluoride is absorbed, transported and deposited in the bone or developing teeth. The deposited fluoride on the surface of teeth does not allow the action of acids or enzymes. Very less amount of fluoride (1 ppm) is required for this purpose.

Route of administration: Route of administration is orally and topically. Drinking water (0.5 to 1 ppm), fruit juice (1 ppm), sodium fluoride tablets or solution, 2.2 mg or topical application of 2 % solution.

A wide range of therapeutic fluoride concentrations are used as topical agents to prevent caries

Method	Fluoride concentration (ppm)
Dentifrices, adult	1000-1500
Dentifrices, children	250-500
Mouth rinse,	230
Self-applied gels or rinses, prescription	5000

Fluoride is considered to be the most effective caries-inhibiting agent, and almost all toothpastes today contain fluoride in one form or the other. The most common form is sodium fluoride (NaF), but mono-fluoro-phosphate (MFP) and stannous fluoride (SnF) are also used. The fluoride amount in toothpaste is usually between 0.10 - 0.15%. Fluoride is most beneficial when the mouth is not rinsed with water after tooth brushing. In this way a bigger amount of fluoride is retained in the oral cavity. Toothpastes are the main vehicles for fluoride. The combined therapeutic and cosmetic mouthwashes usually also contain fluoride, but in a non-therapeutic dose. However, there are fluoride-rinses with higher fluoride concentrations.

There are three main theories considering the positive action of fluoride in the prevention of caries.

1. It is claimed that fluoride, incorporated into the enamel during tooth development in the form of fluorhydroxyapatite (FAP), reduces the solubility of the apatite salt. This theory

implies that "caries resistance", once obtained, will last always. And that fluoride provided during the mineralisation of the teeth is significantly more effective than when given later on. This theory has some draw backs since individuals who are born and raised in an area with fluoridated water, and therefore have their teeth mineralised under optimum fluoride conditions; quickly achieve a caries incidence characteristic of their new location if they leave the fluoridated area. Too much fluoride during tooth development can cause dental fluorosis.

2.   It is also suggested that fluoride has anti-bacterial action. In an acidic environment, if fluoride is present, hydrogen fluoride (HF) is formed. HF is an undissociated, weak acid that can penetrate the bacterial cell membrane. The entry of HF into the alkaline cytoplasmic compartments results in dissociation of HF to H and F. This has two separate, major effects on the physiology of the cell. The first is that the released F interacts with cellular constituents, including various F-sensitive enzymes. The second effect is an acidification of the cytoplasmic compartment caused by the released protons. Normally protons are pumped out of the cell, but fluoride inhibits these processes. The decreased intracellular pH will make the environment less favourable for many of the essential enzymes required for cell growth.

3.   Today, the most important anti-caries effect is claimed to be due to the formation of calcium fluoride (CaF_2) in plaque and on the enamel surface during and after rinsing or brushing with fluoride. CaF_2 serves as a fluoride reservoir. When the pH drops, fluoride and calcium are released into the plaque fluid. Fluoride diffuses with the acid from plaque into the enamel pores and forms fluoroapatite (FAP). FAP incorporated in the enamel surface is more resistant to a subsequent acid attack since the critical pH of FAP (pH = 4.5) is lower than that of hydroxyapatite (HA) (pH = 5.5). Fluoride decreases the demineralisation and increases the remineralisation of the enamel between pH 4.5 - 5.5, and hence the demineralisation period is shortened.

8.2.2 Polishing Agents

Dentifrices contain agents for cleaning tooth surfaces and providing polishing effect on the cleaned teeth. These agents are abrasive in nature. They are responsible for physically removing plaque and debris. Examples include dicalcium phosphate, sodium metaphosphate, calcium pyrophosphate, calcium carbonate and calcium monohydrogen phosphate. Pumice is too abrasive for daily use in a dentifrice.

8.2.3 Desensitising Agents

Desensitising agents reduce the pain in sensitive teeth caused by cold, heat or touch. These products should be non-abrasive and should not be used on a regular basis unless directed by a dentist. Examples include strontium chloride and zinc chloride.

8.2.4 Anti-calculus Agents

The crystal growth inhibitors have been most extensively tested clinically. These agents act by delaying dental plaque calcification, thereby promoting plaque removal with normal tooth brushing.

8.2.5 Whitening Agents

Whitening toothpastes do not lighten the colour of the tooth structure; they simply remove surface stains with abrasives or special chemical or polishing agents, or prevent stain formation

8.2.6 Pumice

Pumice is a substance of volcanic origin, produced when lava with a very high content of water and gases is thrown out of a volcano. As the gas bubbles escape from the lava, it becomes frothy. When this lava cools and hardens, it results in a very light rock material filled with tiny bubbles of gas. It consists mainly of complex silicates of aluminum, potassium, and sodium. It is very light, hard, rough, porous, grayish mass. It is odourless and stable in air.

8.3 Preparation and Assay of Some Important Anti-caries Agents

1. Sodium Fluoride : NaF   Mol. Wt. 41.99

It contains not less than 98.5 percent and not more than 100.5 percent of NaF, calculated with reference to the dried substance.

Preparation

It is prepared by reacting hydrofluoric acid with sodium carbonate. Sodium fluoride being not very soluble precipitates out.

$$2HF + Na_2CO_3 \rightarrow 2NaF + H_2O + CO_2\uparrow$$

The precipitate is contaminated with fluorosilicate and the acid salt. It is made alkaline to phenolphthalein with sodium carbonate and then heated to neutralise the acid salt and decompose the fluorosilicate.

$$Na_2SiF_6 + 2H_2O \rightarrow 2NaF + 4HF + SiO_2$$

Assay

It is assayed by non-aqueous titration method.

Weigh accurately about 80 mg of sodium fluoride and add a mixture of 5 ml of acetic anhydride and 20 ml of anhydrous glacial acetic acid to it. Heat to dissolve, cool, add 20 ml of dioxan and titrate with 0.1M perchloric acid using crystal violet solution as an indicator until green colour is produced. Carry out a blank determination and make any necessary corrections.

Each ml of 0.1M perchloric acid is equivalent to 0.004199 of NaF.

Uses

1. It is used as a preventive for dental caries because of its fluoride ion content. 1.5-3.0 ppm (equivalent to 0.7-1.3 ppm of fluoride ion) in drinking water, 2% solution as a topical application to the teeth is the common means of providing fluoride. Sodium fluoride because of its fluoride ions is an important agent in dental practice for retarding or preventing dental caries.

2. Flouride ion enters the enamel of teeth and becomes part of the enamel structure and thus becomes effective.

2. Stannous Fluoride: SnF_2 **Mol. Wt. : 156.69**

It contains not less than 71.2 percent of stannous (Sn^{2+}) ions and not less than 22.3 percent and not more than 22.5 percent of fluoride, calculated with reference to the dried substance.

Preparation

Stannous fluoride is prepared by heating stannous oxide with gaseous hydrofluoric acid in the absence of oxygen

$$SnO + 2HF \rightarrow SnF_2 + H_2O$$

Assay

Pipette 20 ml of each standard preparation and the assay preparation into separate plastic beakers. Add 20 ml of buffer solution into each beaker. Concomitantly measure the potential of the solutions from the standard preparations and assay preparation using a pH meter equipped with a fluoride specific ion indicating electrode and a calomel reference electrode.

Plot the logarithms of the fluoride ion concentrations, in μg per ml of the standard preparations versus potential, in mV. Determine the concentration, C, in μg per ml, of fluoride ion in the assay preparation from the measured potential of the assay preparation. Calculate the percentage of fluoride by the formula.

$$125 \ C/W$$

Where C is the concentration of fluoride determined in assay preparation and W is the weight of the stannous fluoride taken.

Uses

1. It is used as a preventive for dental caries.
2. A freshly prepared 8% solution is used at 6 to 12 month intervals.

3. Zinc chloride: $ZnCl_2$ **Mol. Wt. : 136.29.**

It contains not less than 95 percent and not more than 100.5 percent of $ZnCl_2$.

Properties

A white or practically white, crystalline powder; odourless; very deliquescent.

Preparation

It is prepared by heating granulated zinc with hydrochloric acid. When evolution of hydrogen ceases, the solution is filtered and evaporated to dryness

$$Zn + 2 HCl \rightarrow ZnCl_2 + H_2 \uparrow$$

Assay

It is assayed by complexometry using strong ammonia–ammonium chloride solution as buffer, eriochrome black T solution as indicator and titrating with 0.1M disodium edetate.

$$ZnCl_2 + C_{10}H_{14}N_2Na_2O_8 \rightarrow C_{10}H_{14}N_2Na_2Zn + 2NaCl$$

Weight accurately about 3 g of $ZnCl_2$ dissolve in 125 ml of water, add 3 g of ammonium chloride and make up the volume to 250 ml with water. To 25 ml of the resulting solution add 100 ml of water and 10 ml of strong ammonia-ammonium chloride solution. Titrate with 0.1M disodium edetate using eriochrome black T solution as an indicator until a deep blue colour is produced.

Each ml of 0.1 M disodium edetate is equivalent to 0.01363 g of $ZnCl_2$.

Uses

1. It is used as an antiseptic astringent to the skin and mucous membrane as a 0.5 – 2.0% solution.
2. It ranks very low among disinfectants.
3. It is used as an active ingredient to prepare magnesia cements for dental fillings and certain mouthwashes.
4. It is also used as dentin desensitizer, topically as a 10% solution to the teeth.

4. Calcium Carbonate (Precipitated Chalk) : $CaCO_3$ **Mol. Wt. : 100.1**

Calcium Carbonate contains not less than 98.0 per cent and not more than 100.5 per cent of $CaCO_3$, calculated on the dried basis.

Properties

A fine, white, microcrystalline powder practically insoluble in water and in ethanol (95 per cent); slightly soluble in water containing carbon dioxide or any ammonium salt. It is soluble with effervescence in dilute acids.

Preparation

It is prepared by mixing boiling solution of calcium chloride and sodium carbonate.

$$CaCl_2 + Na_2CO_3 \rightarrow CaCO_3 + 2\ NaCl$$

The precipitate is collected on filter, washed with boiling water and dried.

Assay

Weigh accurately about 0.1 g of $CaCO_3$ and dissolve in 3 ml of dilute hydrochloric acid and 10 ml of water. Boil for 10 minutes, cool, dilute to 50 ml with water. Titrate with 0.05 M disodium edetate. Within a few ml of the expected end-point, add 8 ml of sodium hydroxide solution and 0.1 g of calcon mixture and continue the titration until the colour of the solution changes from pink to a full blue colour.

1 ml of 0.05 M disodium edetate is equivalent to 0.005004 g of $CaCO_3$.

Uses

The precipitated chalk is used externally as dentifrices because it has mild abrasive quality. It forms common ingredients of tooth powder and tooth paste.

5. Dibasic Calcium Phosphate (Calcium Hydrogen Phosphate)

$CaHPO_4$; Mol. Wt. 136.1 (anhydrous)

$CaHPO_4, 2H_2O$; Mol. Wt. 172.1 (dihydrate)

Dibasic Calcium Phosphate is anhydrous or contains two molecules of water of hydration. Dibasic Calcium Phosphate contains not less than 98.0 per cent and not more than 105.0 per cent of $CaHPO_4$ (for anhydrous material) or of $CaHPO_4, 2H_2O$ (for the dihydrate).

Properties

A white crystalline; odourless powder.

Preparation

It may be prepared by reacting natural solution of calcium chloride with disodium hydrogen phosphate.

$$CaCl_2 + Na_2HPO_4 \rightarrow CaHPO_4 + 2NaCl$$

Assay

Weigh accurately about 0.3 g of dibasic calcium phosphate and dissolve in a mixture of 5 ml of water and 1 ml of 7 M hydrochloric acid, add 25.0 ml of 0.1 M disodium edetate and dilute to 200 ml with water. Neutralise with strong ammonia solution, add 10 ml of ammonia buffer pH 10.0 and 50 mg of mordant black 11mixtures and titrate the excess of disodium edetate with 0.1 M zinc sulphate.

1 ml of 0.1 M disodium edetate is equivalent to 0.01361 g of $CaHPO_4$ or 0.01721 g of $CaHPO_4, 2H_2O$.

Uses

1. This calcium salt has 1:1 ratio of calcium to phosphorus and is most frequently recommended for oral administration as an electrolyte replenishes.
2. As a salt it supplies both calcium and phosphourus which is required for the growth in children, pregent women and lactating mothers.
3. Externally it is used as dentrifices having cleaning action the moderate abrasive quality makes it suitable for tooth paste and tooth powders.

Question Bank

1. Write notes on-
    (a) Anticaries agents.
    (b) Calcium compounds as dentifrices.
    (c) Preparation, properties, uses and assay of sodium fluoride
    (d) Role of fluoride as anticaries agent.
2. Discuss mechanism of action of anti-caries agents.
3. Explain the role of fluoride and phosphate in tooth decay.
4. Explain the role of fluorides in tooth decay.
5. Dentifrices and desensitising agents.
6. Write about dentifrices.

✍ ✍ ✍

Chapter 9...

Gases and Vapours

Contents ...

9.1   Introduction

9.2   Oxygen

9.3   Nitrogen

9.4   Nitrous Oxide

9.5   Carbon Dioxide

9.6   Helium

9.7   Ammonia

•   Question Bank

9.1 Introduction

The principal gases used in pharmacy are **nitrogen, oxygen, carbon dioxide, argon, hydrogen, helium**, **ammonia** and **acetylene**; although a huge variety of gases and mixtures are available in gas cylinders. The industry producing these gases is known as the industrial gases industry, which is seen as also encompassing the supply of equipment and technology to produce and use gases.

The known chemical elements which are, or can be obtained from natural resources and which are gaseous are hydrogen, nitrogen, oxygen, fluorine, chlorine, plus the noble gases; and are collectively referred to by chemists as the "elemental gases".

These elements are all primordial, apart from the noble gas radon which is a trace radioisotope but which does occur naturally, albeit only from radioactive decay. (It is not known if any synthetic elements with atomic number above 108 are gases.)

The gases which are used as inhalants include oxygen, carbon dioxide, nitrous oxide, helium, nitrogen.

9.2 Oxygen

Molecular formula: O_2 **Molecular Weight :** 32.0

Oxygen contains not less than 99.0 per cent v/v of O_2.

Properties

Oxygen is a colourless, odourless, tasteless gas having a density of 1.1. It is chemically reactive and primarily functions as an oxidising agent. It dissolves in about 32 volumes of water and 36 volumes of alcohol at 1 atmospheric pressure. It does not combine directly with halogen and inert gases.

Preparation

Oxygen is manufactured by fractional distillation of liquid air. Nitrogen (boiling point 196°C) tends to distil out first, leaving oxygen (boiling point 183°c) behind. Oxygen is also manufactured by the electrolysis of water.

Assay

It may be assayed by geometric method, which uses a nitrometer which consists of a measuring tube and a balancing tube connected by a rubber tubing. The absorbing agent is a solution of ammonium chloride and ammonium hydroxide. Decrease in the volume of gas is measured that gets reduced under standard conditions of temperature and pressure.

Storage

Store under pressure in metal cylinders of the type conforming to the appropriate safety regulations. Valves and taps should not be lubricated with oil or grease.

Labelling

The cylinder should carry a label stating "Oxygen". In addition, "Oxygen" or the symbol "O_2" should be painted on the shoulder of the cylinder. The shoulder of the metal cylinder should be painted white and the remainder should be painted black. The WHO (World Health Organization) suggests that the cylinder should be of green colour. Since oxygen supports rapid combustion, smoking and open flames must be prevented nearby.

Role of Oxygen

1. In the human body, oxygen is absorbed by the blood from the lungs and transported to all the cells where oxygen is exchanged for carbon dioxide, the waste product of metabolic respiration.
2. Oxygen plays a vital in the metabolism of living organisms. The only living cells that do not need oxygen are some anaerobic bacteria that obtain energy from other metabolic processes.
3. The nutrient compounds, inside the cell, are oxidised through complex biochemical processes. This oxidation is the main source of energy for most animals.
4. The by-products of cellular respiration are carbon dioxide and water (exhaled air has a relative humidity of 100%), which are eliminated through the lungs.
5. Cellular respiration: molecular oxygen is essential for cellular respiration in all aerobic organisms. Oxygen is used as an electron acceptor in mitochondria to generate chemical energy.
6. Transport of oxygen is facilitated by haemoglobin, a constituent of blood. Oxygen combines with haemoglobin.

$$Hb + O_2 = HbO_2$$

Where in, Hb = deoxyhaemoglobin; HbO_2 = oxyhaemoglobin

Uses

1. Oxygen is required by all aerobic organisms. In blood, oxygen combines with haemoglobin and is carried to all the cells of the body.

2. It is widely used in the treatment of hypoxia.

3. It is usually administered by means of an oxygen mask in concentrations ranging from 40-100% oxygen.

4. It gives relief in the treatment of anoxia.

5. Oxygen is useful in a treatment of carbon monoxide poisoning.

6. It is used in radiation therapy in cancer treatment.

7. In industry, oxygen is used in oxyacetylene flame required for welding or cutting metals.

8. Liquid oxygen is used as a fuel in rocket technology.

9.3 Nitrogen

Molecular formula : N_2 **Molecular weight :** 14

Properties

Nitrogen is colourless, odourless and tasteless gas. Nitrogen is inert chemically, and does not react with ordinary reagents. It is sparingly soluble in water. At $0°$ C, 100 volumes of water absorb 2.4 volumes of nitrogen and at $20°$ C, 1.6 volume of the same. It is condensed to be a colourless liquid which boils at $-195.8°$ C at ordinary atmospheric pressure and solidifies to a white snow like mass that melts at $-209.8°$ C.

Preparation

It is manufactured by the fractional distillation of liquid air. Because of its inert nature, it may be used to protect chemicals and pharmaceutical products from air oxidation. Such oxidation-sensitive products are filled in the vessels or containers containing nitrogen gases.

Assay

The percentage of nitrogen in the given sample of air is determined by removing other gases and measuring the volume of the remaining inert gases and nitrogen. Carbon dioxide is removed from air by passing it through a solution of NaOH, while oxygen is removed by copper turnings which form a non-volatile oxide.

The percentage of nitrogen in a compound is determined by Kjeldalh's method.

Uses

1. It is used to prevent oxidation degradation of pharmaceuticals (e.g. cod liver oil, olive oil) because of its inert nature.
2. It is also used to replace air in containers for parenterals and solution for topical application. Due to inert nature it increases the shelf life of products.
3. Ascorbic acid injections are to be filled under an inert atmosphere of nitrogen.

9.4 Nitrous Oxide

Molecular formula: N_2O **Molecular Weight :** 44.0

Nitrous Oxide contains not less than 98.0 per cent v/v of N_2O.

Properties

It is a colourless and odourless gas. It also called as laughing gas as it produces an exhilarating effect when inhaled. Nitrous oxide has a sweetish taste. It dissolves in water and is soluble in alcohol.

Preparation

Nitrous oxide is prepared by thermal decomposition of ammonium nitrate. This gas is purified by washing with sodium chromate, sodium hydroxide and water and filled in cylinder.

$$NH_4NO_3 \rightarrow 2H_2O + N_2O$$

Assay

Nitrous oxide may be assayed, by the gasometric method where liquid oxygen is used as an absorbing agent. A known volume (50 ml) of the gas is allowed to cool in liquid oxygen for about 20 minutes. The uncondensed gas is taken out in an eudiometer tube and measured. The uncondensed gases which may be nitrogen with traces of oxygen should not exceed 1%.

Storage

It is stored under pressure in metal cylinders of the type conforming to the appropriate safety regulations and at a temperature not exceeding 37°C.

Labelling

The cylinder should be painted blue and labeled stating "Nitrous Oxide". In addition, "Nitrous Oxide" or the symbol "N_2O" should be painted on the shoulder of the cylinder.

Uses

1. It is used by inhalation for surgical procedures of short duration like dental extraction, treatment of boils etc.
2. It has anesthetic and analgesic effects.
3. It is also effective in calming psychological patients. It is given by inhalation in concentrations of 60-80% or with oxygen 20-40% as required.

9.5 Carbon Dixoide

Molecular formula : CO_2 **Molecular Weight :** 44.01

Properties

Carbon dioxide is a colourless, odourless gas. It is slightly acidic. It is soluble in water. It does not support combustion.

Preparation

It is obtained when compounds containing carbon like coal, coke oil etc. are burnt with an excess of oxygen.

$$C + O_2 \rightarrow CO_2$$

When carbonate is treated with acid carbon dioxide gas is evolved.

$$CaCO_3 + 2HCl \rightarrow H_2CO_3 + CaCl_2$$

$$H_2CO_3 \rightarrow H_2O + CO_2$$

Assay

It is assayed by gasometric method. The apparatus consists of a nitrometer connected by rubber tubing to a balancing tube. The absorption of 50% potassium hydroxide solution decreases the volume in gases absorbing liquids after correction to standard temperature and pressure with not more than 1 ml of gas remaining in the tube.

$$CO_2 + 2KOH \rightarrow K_2CO_3 + H_2O$$

Role of Carbon dioxide

1. It is readily absorbed and carried by blood, cell and in the plasma.
2. It is also found in the body during metabolic process. Large quantities of carbon dioxide produced is removed by lungs in the exhaled air.
3. The interchange and transport mechanism for carbon dioxide and oxygen takes place in lungs, in tissues and blood.
4. Carbon dioxide is the end product of metabolism in all aerobic organisms.
5. The bicarbonate/carbonic acid ratio is an important determinant of the pH of body fluids. A decreased removal of carbon dioxide can cause respiratory acidosis while increased removal may lead to respiratory alkalosis.
6. The dizziness accompanying the latter condition is experienced during hyperventilation.

Storage and Labeling

It is supplied in a metal cylinder painted grey and has the name and symbol CO_2 stenciled on it.

Use

1. It stimulates respiratory and cardio vascular centre.
2. A mixture of 5% CO_2 with oxygen or up to 10% with air is used in treatment of carbon monoxide poisoning.
3. Useful in treatment of drug addiction.
4. Used to prepare dry ice which is used for minor surgical procedures for destroying tissues or preserving labile products.
5. Used in beverage industry for preparation of concentrated soft drinks.
6. Pharmaceutically it is used to displace air in some parenteral preparation.

9.6 Helium

Molecular formula: He   **Molecular Weight :** 4.002

Properties

Helium is an odourless, tasteless and colorless gas. It is the lightest gas known. It is not in the official pharmacopeia of India. It is official in British Pharmacopoeia. It is sparingly soluble in water. It is chemically inert and possesses zero valency. Its molecules are monoatomic. Helium being non-inflammable, is used for inflating airships.

Preparation

It is found in nature. It is obtained as a by product of liquid air fractional distillation.

Assay

It is assayed by a gasometric method. The official assay of helium depends on its absorption in the liquid oxygen. The unabsorbed gases are pumped off and measured. The volume is then corrected to standard conditions of temperature and pressure. Not less than 98.0 % v/v of the volume taken is recovered.

Storage

It is supplied in metal cylinders under compression at 98% v/v purity. The cylinders are coloured brown. Mixture of oxygen (20 – 21%) and helium (79.80% v/v) and also supplied in cylinders which are painted black on the body and white and brown patches on the shoulders and neck.

Uses

1. It may be used as diluents in oxygen administered in the treatment of respiratory embracement.
2. It is used in the field of cryogenics (i.e. low temperature)
3. It is used as a carrier gas in gas chromatography.

9.7 Ammonia

Molecular formula: NH_3 **Molecular Weight** 17.0

Properties

It is colourless gas with a strong pungent odour. It has a density of 0.7710. It is easily condensed to a liquid (boiling point 33°C) which is used as refrigerating agent. Ammonia is very soluble in water. Its solution is alkaline to litmus. The usual concentrated solution contains 35% ammonia by weight.

Preparation

It is a basic substance and can be prepared in the laboratory by reaction between ammonium salt and a strong base like, $Ca(OH)_2$.

Assay

It is assayed colorimetrically by the yellow colour it gives with Nessler's solution. The ammonia in the ammonium salt is determined by distilling the salt with excess of the NaOH. The distillate is passed into a known volume of standard acid. The excess of standard acid can be determined by back titration with standard alkali. Methyl red is used as an indicator for the titration of ammonia with strong acids.

$$NH_3 + HCl \rightarrow NH_4Cl$$

Each ml of 1N HCl $\cong$ 17.03 mg of NH_3

Use

Respiratory stimulant.

Compound of Ammonia

Ammonia Solution Strong : Strong ammonia solution contains not less than 27.0% w/w and not more than 30.0% w/w of ammonia.

Properties

It appears as a colourless transparent liquid with strong pungent odour. It has a strong alkaline taste. It has a density of 0.90 - .91. It is miscible with water and alcohol.

Assay

It is a simple acid-base titration. An accurately weighed (3.0g) sample is taken in a flask with 50.0 ml 1 N sulphuric acid. The excess of acid is titrated with 1 N sodium hydroxide solution using methyl red as an indicator.

Each ml of 1N H_2SO_4 $\cong$ 17.03 mg of NH_3

Uses

It may be used as an antacid and respiratory stimulant.

Question Bank

1. Give properties and storage conditions of oxygen, carbon dioxide and nitrous oxide.

2. Discuss properties, uses and role of oxygen.

3. Write in detail about oxygen.

4. Discuss the role of oxygen in biological system.

5. Give the properties, uses and method of assay of ammonia.

6. Explain the role of oxygen, carbon dioxide in human body.

7. Properties, uses and method of assay of oxygen.

8. Give the method of preparation, properties and uses of nitrous oxide.

9. Give properties, uses and storage conditions of following inorganic gases.

   (i) Oxygen, (ii) Nitrogen, (iii) Nitrous oxide

   ✍   ✍   ✍

Chapter 10...

Miscellaneous Agents

Contents ...

10.1 Expectorants

10.2 Radio-opaque Medium

10.3 Antidotes

10.4 Antidepressants

10.5 Cytotoxic Agents

•   Question Bank

10.1 Expectorants

Expectorants (from the Latin *expectorare*, to expel from the chest) are drugs which enhance the secretion of the sputum by the air passages so that it is easier to remove the phlegm through coughing. They are used in cough mixtures for this purpose, they act either by increasing the bronchiole secretion or by making it less viscous (mucolytic agents). Drugs such as ipecacuanha in small doses act as stimulant expectorants. They irritate the lining of the stomach whose reflex stimulates the production of sputum by the glands in the bronchial mucous membrane.

Classification of Expectorants

(a) Sedative type e.g., Ipecac.

(b) Stimulant type e.g., Eucalyptus, lemon, anise, terpin hydrate.

Potassium iodide stimulates the gastric mucosa and increases the bronchiole secretion. Ammonium chloride acts like potassium iodide but, is less potent. Antimony potassium tartrate is also used as an expectorant.

1. Ammonium Chloride

Molecular formula: (NH_4Cl),   **Molecular Weight** 53.5

Ammonium chloride contains not less than 99.0 per cent and not more than 100.5 per cent of NH_4Cl, calculated on the dried basis.

Properties

Colourless crystals or a white, crystalline powder, odourless, highly soluble in water. Solutions of ammonium chloride are mildly acidic and freely soluble in glycerine.

Preparation

It is prepared by the interaction of ammonia gas with hydrochloric acid. The solution is evaporated to dryness.

$$NH_3 + HCl \rightarrow NH_4Cl$$

It may also be prepared by treating ammonia gas liquors with lime and the liberated ammonia is passed into hydrochloric acid.

Assay

It is assayed by simple acid base titration. Weigh accurately about 0.1 g of ammonium chloride, dissolve in 20 ml of water and add a mixture of 5 ml of formaldehyde solution, previously neutralised to dilute phenolphthalein solution, and 20 ml of water. After 2 minutes, titrate slowly with 0.1 M sodium hydroxide using a further 0.2 ml of dilute phenolphthalein solution as an indicator.

1 ml of 0.1 M sodium hydroxide is equivalent to 0.005349 g of NH_4Cl.

Storage

It is stored in a tightly closed container.

Uses

1. Ammonium chloride is used as an expectorant in cough medicine.
2. Its expectorant action is caused by irritative action on the bronchial mucosa. This causes the production of excess respiratory tract fluid which presumably is easier to cough up.
3. Ammonium salts are an irritant to the gastric mucosa and may induce nausea and vomiting.
4. Ammonium chloride is used as a systemic acidifying agent in the treatment of severe metabolic alkalosis, in oral acid loading test to diagnose distal renal tubular acidosis, to maintain urine at an acid pH in the treatment of some urinary-tract disorders.

2. Potassium Iodide

Molecular formula: (KI),   **Molecular Weight** 166.0

Potassium Iodide contains not less than 99.0 per cent and not more than 100.5 per cent of KI, calculated on the dried basis.

Properties

Colourless crystals or a white powder. It is odourless having saline and bitter taste. It is soluble in water and glycerine.

Preparation

It is prepared by adding excess of iodine to the solution of potassium iodide. It is purified and iodates are formed. The potassium iodate is reduced to potassium iodide with carbon.

$$6KOH + 3I_2 \rightarrow 5KI + KIO_3 + 3H_2O$$
$$KIO_3 + 3C \rightarrow KI + 3CO$$

Assay

Weigh accurately about 0.35g of potassium iodide, dissolve in about 10 ml of water, add 35 ml of hydrochloric acid and 5 ml of chloroform. Titrate with 0.05 M potassium iodate until the purple colour of iodine disappears from the chloroform. Add the last portion of the iodate solution dropwise and agitate vigorously and continuously. Allow to stand for 5 minutes. If any colour develops in the chloroform layer continue the titration until the chloroform is decolorised.

1 ml of 0.05 M potassium iodate is equivalent to 0.0166 g of KI.

Storage

Store protected from light and moisture.

Uses

1. Used internally for supplying iodine for the treatment of thyroid deficiency.

2. Used as an expectorant in cough mixture.

3. It also has mild antifungal activity. It is also used for preparing reagents containing complex iodides.

10.2 Radio-opaque Medium

Radio-contrast agents are a type of medical contrast medium used to improve the visibility of internal bodily structures in X-ray-based imaging techniques such as computed tomography (CT), radiography, and fluoroscopy. Radio-contrast agents are typically iodine or barium compounds. When an agent improves visibility of an area, it is called "contrast enhancing".

Inorganic compounds like barium sulphate and some bismuth compounds thus are useful as radio – opaque contrast media for diagnostic use.

The diagnostic study of bones is carried out using X-rays, as the soft tissues are permeable to the passage of X-rays (as the tissues are mostly composed of elements of low atomic numbers like carbon, hydrogen, oxygen and nitrogen) and hence cause darkening of X-rays film. The bony structure casts shadow on the film as the cones contain elements having high atomic number like calcium and phosphorus. As a result bony tissues can be distinguished on an exposed X-ray film.

1. Barium Sulphate

Molecular formula: $(BaSO_4)$,   **Molecular Weight:** 233.4

Barium Sulphate contains not less than 97.5 per cent and not more than 100.5 per cent of $BaSO_4$.

Properties

It is an odourless, fine, heavy, white powder, free from gritty particles. The substance exists as a water insoluble white powder that is made into slurry with water and administered directly into the *gastrointestinal tract*. Barium sulphate is an insoluble white powder typically used for enhancing contrast in the GI tract.

Preparation

Barium sulphate for the rentogen ray purpose (X – ray) is prepared by precipitating barium ions from cold dilute solutions of barium salt with dilute sulphuric acid.

$$Ba(OH)_2 + H_2SO_4 \rightarrow BaSO_4 + 2H_2O\downarrow$$

$$BaCl_2 + H_2SO_4 \rightarrow BaSO_4 + 2HCl\downarrow$$

The precipitated salt is thoroughly washed, dried and then screened. Industrial grade barium sulphate is a byproduct of many industries e.g. during the manufacture of H_2O_2 from $BaO_2.8H_2O$. It can also be prepared by the action of dilute H_2SO_4 on BaS (barium sulphide).

Assay

It is assayed gravimetrically.

Barium sulphate and barium sulphate suspension are assayed by fusion of the known weight of compound with sodium carbonate and potassium carbonate at $1000°$ C for 15 minutes. It is cooled, suspended in water and decanted. The residue is washed with 2% sodium carbonate solutions aqueous. Dilute hydrochloric acid is added followed by potassium dichromate, urea and ammonium acetate. The suspension is digested at 80 - 85°C for 16 minutes and then filtered through sintered glass crucible. The residue is washed with potassium dichromate solution followed by water and the contents are weighed after drying at $105°$ C.

Uses

1. Barium sulphate is mainly used in the imaging of the digestive system
2. Depending on how it is to be administered the compound is mixed with water, thickeners, de-clumping agents and flavourings to prepare the contrast agent.
3. As the barium sulphate does not dissolve, this type of contrast agent is an opaque white mixture. It is only used in the digestive tract.
4. It is usually swallowed or administered as an enema. After the examination, it leaves the body with the faeces.

10.3 Antidotes

Antidotes are the agents which are used to reverse stop or counteract the action of poisons. Cyanide produces a rapid onset of toxicity which must be vigorously and immediately treated to prevent toxic syndrome. To obtain better protection, a series of newer antidotes either alone or in adjunction with the conventional treatments have been examined.

On the basis of their mechanism of action, antidotes can be classified as follows:

1. **Physiological antidote :** It acts by producing the effect opposite to that produced by the poison which means to counteract the effect of poison physiologically. Example : Sodium nitrite is used to treat cyanide poisoning.

2. **Chemical antidote :** It acts by combining with the poison and thus, changes the chemical nature such that the poison cannot act anymore.

   Example : Sodium thiosulphate is used to treat cyanide poisoning.

3. **Mechanical antidote :** It acts by preventing the absorption of poison in the body or expelling out the poison by elimination through urine or emesis.

   Example: Activated charcoal.

Cyanide Poisoning

It normally occurs when taken internally for suicidal purpose or accidently. Cyanide ion combined with ferric ion of cytochrome oxidase as the enzyme is responsible for electron transfer reaction. This leads to stoppage of cellular respiration and metabolic reactions immediately.

In cyanide poisoning, sodium nitrite and sodium thiosulphate injection are given to counteract the effect of the cyanide poison.

Sodium thiosulphate reacts with cyanide ion and converts into sodium thiocyanide which is less toxic than cyanide. While sodium nitrite reacts with ferrous iron and hemoglobin and convert into ferric iron of methahemoglobin and thus reduces the concentration of cyanide ion

1. **Sodium Thiosulphate**

   Molecular formula: $Na_2S_2O_3,5H_2O$,   **Molecular Weight:** 248.2

   Sodium Thiosulphate contains not less than 99.0 per cent and not more than 101.0 per cent of $Na_2S_2O_3,5H_2O$.

Properties

Colourless large crystals or a coarse, crystalline powder; odourless; deliquescent in moist air and effloresces in dry air at temperature above 33°. It dissolves in its water of crystallisation at about 49° C.

Preparation

It can be prepared by boiling sodium sulphite with sulphur.

$$Na_2SO_3 + S \rightarrow Na_2S_2O_3$$

Assay

Weigh accurately about 0.5 g, dissolve in 20 ml of water and titrate with 0.05 M iodine using starch solution, added towards the end of the titration, as indicator.

1 ml of 0.05 M iodine is equivalent to 0.02482 g of $Na_2S_2O_3,5H_2O$.

Storage

Store in a clean and dry place, protected from moisture.

Uses

1. It has been included in pharmacopeia as an antidote for cyanide poisoning.
2. For this purpose a 10% w/v solution is used intravenously although a 2.98% w/v solution is isotonic with serum.
3. Sodium thiosulphate is also a very important reducing agent and is used as a standard titrant in iodimetric titration.

2. Sodium Nitrite

Molecular Formula : $NaNO_2$ **Molecular Weight:** 69.0

It contains not less than 97% and not more than 101.0% $NaNO_2$ with reference to substance dried over silica gel.

Properties

Sodium nitrite occurs in the form of white granular powder or as a white crystal having a saline taste. It is water soluble; sparingly soluble in alcohol. When exposed to air it deliquesces and gets slowly oxidised to sodium nitrate. It is easily decomposed by acidification with dilute sulphuric acid. Chemically it acts as reducing agent and gets oxidised in acidic medium.

Preparation

It is manufactured by many methods. The most suitable method involves passing of nitrogen oxide gas (NO) obtained during the catalytic oxidation of ammonia and oxygen in sodium carbonate solution. The solution is concentrated to crystallise out the product.

$$2Na_2CO_3 + 4NO + O_2 \rightarrow 4NaNO_2 + 2CO_2\uparrow$$

Assay

Weigh accurately 1 gm sample and dissolve in 100 ml water solution. In a volumetric flask take 40 ml of 0.1 mol/ml $KMnO_4$ solution, add 100 ml water, and 5 ml conc. H_2SO_4. In this add 10 ml of solution A. Shake and allow the mixture to stand for 5 min, then add 25 ml of 0.05 M oxalic acid solution and warm the mixture at 80°C and titrate the excess oxalic acid against 0.02 M $KMnO_4$, while hot. Perform a blank along side.

1 ml of 0.02 M $KMnO_4$ $\cong$ 3.4498 mg $NaNO_2$

Uses

1. In medicine, it was used as a vasodilator but, has been now largely replaced by organic nitrites and nitrates, nitroglycerin, isosorbide dinitrate.
2. Medicinally it is mainly used as an antidote in cyanide poisoning and has a hypotensive effect.
3. It has relaxant action on smooth muscles.
4. Rusting of surgical instruments is prevented when immersed in a dilute solution.
5. It is also used as a food preservative.

10.4 Antidepressants

Antidepressants work by balancing brain neurotransmitter levels in the brain to ease depression. Drugs used for the treatment of major depressive disorder are listed below.

Classification of antidepressants

(1) Tricyclic antidepressants (TCAs)

(2) Tetracyclic antidepressants

(3) Selective serotonin re-uptake inhibitors (SSRIs)

(4) Serotonin and nor epinephrine re-uptake inhibitors (SNRIs)

(5) Serotonin receptor modulators (SRMs)

(6) Monoamine oxidase inhibitors (MAOIs)

(7) Lithium Salts

Mechanism of Action of Antidepressants

Antidepressants enhance the serotonergic, noradrenergic and dopaminergic transmission in the brain. These effects are achieved by inhibition of serotonin or noradrenaline reuptake from the synpatic cleft into the neuron (TCAs, SSRIs, SNRIs, NSSRIs), by inhibition of the monoamine metabolism *via* the monoamine oxidase (tranylcypromine, moclobemide) or by blocking specific receptors, for example presynaptic noradrenaline-α^2 receptors and serotonergic 5-HT2- and 5-HT3 receptors. This enhances the stimulation of 5-HT1A autoreceptors (mirtazapine). With chronic administration of antidepressants the monoamine receptors adapt their responsiveness by down-regulation of noradrenaline-β receptors, noradrenaline-$\alpha2$ receptors and serotonin-5-HT1A autoreceptors and by up-regulation of noradrenaline-$\alpha1$ receptors and dopamine-D2 receptors. Altogether these effects lead to a modulation of second messenger systems and gene expression that causes the antidepressive effect with a delay of 3-6 weeks

Classification of Antidepressants

(1) Selective serotenine reuptake inhibitor. Eg. Citalopram

(2) Serotonine norepinephrine reuptake inhibitor. Eg. Duloxetine

(3) Tricyclic antidepressant. Eg. Amitriptyline

(4) Monoamine oxidate inhibitor. Eg. Selegiline

1. Lithium Carbonate

Molecular formula : Li_2CO_3,   **Molecular Weight:** 73.9

Lithium Carbonate contains not less than 98.5 per cent and not more than 100.5 per cent of Li_2CO_3

Properties

A white, crystalline powder. It is odourless but has slight alkaline taste.

Preparation

It may be prepared by adding ammonium carbonate to a solution of lithium salt.

$$Li_2SO_4 + (NH_4)_2CO_3 \rightarrow Li_2CO_3 + (NH_4)_2SO_4$$

Assay

Weigh accurately about 0.5 g of sample and dissolve in 25.0 ml of 1 M hydrochloric acid and titrate against 1 M sodium hydroxide using methyl orange solution as an indicator.

1 ml of 1 M hydrochloric acid is equivalent to 0.03695 g of Li_2CO_3.

Storage

Store in a cool and dry places, protected from moisture.

Uses

1. It is used both in treatment and prevention of manic depressive disease.
2. It is not suitable for children.
3. The action of lithium is slow and it may be given along with anti psychotic drug for some days for immediate response in case of an acute manic attack.
4. It is also used in the treatment of bipolar disorder, mood disorders.
5. A number of salts of lithium are used as mood stabilising drug, depression and mania.

10.5 Cytotoxic Agents

Cancer chemotherapy is the treatment of cancer with one or more cytotoxic, antineoplastic drugs, (Chemotherapeutic Agents). It is often used in combination with other treatments such as radiation therapy or surgery.

Types of Cancer

1. Skin Cancer
2. Blood Cancer
3. Mouth Cancer
4. Stomach Cancer
5. Breast Cancer
6. Bladder Cancer
7. Lung Cancer
8. Hodgkin's Disease
9. Germ Cell Tumor

Traditionally chemotherapy agent acts by killing cells that divide rapidly which is one of the properties of cancer cells. This means chemotherapy also harms cells that divide rapidly under normal circumstances. Cells in the bone marrow, digestive system and hair follicle are cells commonly affected by chemotherapy.Therefore the side effects of chemotherapy are-

(1) Myelo suprpression i.e., decrease in the production of blood cells causing immune suppression.

(2) Mucositis i.e., inflammation of the living cells of the digestive tract.

(3) Alopecia (hair loss)

1. Cisplatin

Molecular formula : $H_6Cl_2N_2Pt$,   **Molecular Weight:** 300.0

Cisplatin is cis-diamminedichloroplatinum(II). Cisplatin contains not less than 97.0 per cent and not more than 102.0 per cent of $H_6Cl_2N_2Pt$.

Properties

It is composed of yellow powder or orange yellow crystals, slightly soluble in water, sparingly soluble in dimethylformamide and insoluble in alcohol.

Preparation

It is prepared by reducing chloroplatinic acid or its potassium salt with hydrazine when tetra chloroplatinic acid or its salt is obtained. This is treated with ammonium chloride and ammonia mixture which precipitates the cis-isomer. The precipitate is filtered, washed and dried.

$$H_2 Pt Cl_6 + NH_2 . NH_2 \rightarrow H_2PtCl_4 + N_2 + 2HCl$$
$$K_2 Pt Cl_6 + NH_2 . NH_2 \rightarrow K_2PtCl_4 + N_2 + 2HCl$$

Assay

Determined by liquid chromatography.

Test solution: Prepare a 0.05 per cent w/v solution of the substance under examination in normal saline just before use.

Reference solution is a 0.05 per cent w/v solution of cisplatin RS in normal saline.

The chromatographic system is composed of a stainless steel column with dimensions 25 cm × 4.6 mm, packed with strong anion-exchange silica gel (10 µm). The mobile phase is a mixture of 90 volumes of methanol and 10 volumes of normal saline. The flow rate is maintained at 1.2 ml per minute. The spectrophotometer is set at 220 nm, 20µl loop injector. The content of $H_6Cl_2N_2Pt$ is then calculated

Storage

It is protected from light.

Uses

It has been effective in testicular and ovarian tumors for which it is currently used. It is generally administered IV as a short term infusion. In normal saline for treatment of solid maliganinsis

1. Various cancers including some sarcomas. E.g., Small scale lung cancer and ovarian or germ cell tumor

2. Cisplatine is particularly effective against testicular cancer.

3. The cure rate has improved from 10-85%.

4. Its use should be under medical supervision.

Question Bank

1. Give classification of antidotes on the basis of their mechanism of action with examples. Explain mechanism of action of sodium nitrite and sodium thiosulphate intravenous infusion in cyanide poisoning.

2. Discuss sodium thiosulphate as an antidote.

3. Describe the method of preparation, uses and assay of compounds used in cyanide poisoning

4. What are expectorants and emetics? Give their mechanism of action.

   (a) Ammonium chloride   (b) KI

5. Explain the reactions involved in the assay of KI.

6. What are expectorants? Explain the assay of ammonium chloride.

7. What are Radio-opaque contrast medias? Discuss properties and uses of any one agent.

8. Write a note on anti-neoplastic agents.

9. Write a note on expectorants.

10. Describe in details the following inorganic compounds (any 2).

    (a) KI,   (b) $BaSO_4$,   (c) $Na_2S_2O_3$,   (d) NH_4Cl.

11. Describe the principle behind using ammonium chloride as an expectorant. Also mention the reaction involved in its principle and describe the method of assay.

12. Write a note on antidepressants.

13. Give a brief account on radio contrast media.

✎   ✎   ✎